DAVID

quietus /kwʌɪˈiːtəs/ noun

[ORIGIN: Abbreviation of Medieval Latin *quietus est* lit. 'he is quit'.]

1. An acquittance granted on payment of a debt; a receipt. A discharge or release from office or duty.

2. Death regarded as a release from life; something which causes death. A final settlement, an ending.

Stevenson, A et al (2007) *Shorter Oxford English Dictionary.* 6st edn. Oxford University Press.

DEDICATION

To those of you who believed in me … but more importantly … to the few who didn't.

ACKNOWLEDGEMENTS

Thank you to all the proofreaders who helped make this happen, but especially to Heather, for always wanting more.

The blood, oh my God, the blood...

CHAPTER ONE

Arriving

I rubbed the heavy crust of tear-filled sleep from my sticky eyes and focussed towards the seascape. We were approaching the harbour - my parents having driven through the night to get here, ready for a new life in Jersey - a place that had always been their favourite holiday destination, and mine too, although I had not been here since I was twelve-years-old.

I peeled my face away from the tiny passenger window and tried hopelessly to find a more comfortable position, next to the boxes, in the already cramped rear of my parents' black *Audi TTRS*. I had only turned seventeen a few months back and learning to drive was the last of my concerns, my time instead taken up by my girlfriend, before she killed herself.

Sophie had slit her wrists, right there in front of me. She had taken a kitchen knife and damn near taken off both her hands. Blood had spilled onto the beige tiles of the kitchen floor and as she turned around and stumbled over the sink, the unwashed dishes were also splashed red. I had instantly frozen and merely observed as Sophie turned back towards me and sank to her knees. At that point I finally sprung to life, but not before urinating myself. That vision of Sophie, my girlfriend of two years, slicing through tendons and bone in her tiny fragile wrists, would haunt me forever.

"There's the port," I heard my father say. My mother gave his hand a squeeze. "In just over four hours we'll be there, away from this madness," he continued, looking mournfully at her.

My mother turned and looked blankly at me - my knees pulled to my chest as I cowering in the back seat. Her eyes were red and swollen. Her dyed, auburn hair matted against her cheeks. For the first time in years, and despite her cosmetic attempts, she looked her actual age. She quietly wept before wiping her nose with the back of her pale, delicate hand and focused back towards the port. She sniffed twice and then there was silence.

.   .   .

I had never been too sure about boats, but my nervous stomach, queasy at every opportunity, held firm on this occasion. I had even managed to sit up at the table whilst my mother and father snacked on a shared sandwich and coffee. I couldn't face either, but was pleased that I could at least join them.

I hoped that through all of this, I might find out more about my parents, about their secretive lives and that maybe we could all become closer. Our move to Jersey was surely a positive thing: I hoped they did it because they cared and wanted to take me away from the impending funeral and the need to deal with the environment that surrounded and reminded me of Sophie, and her death. That's what I wanted - for them to care about me for once. *Pathetic really.* In the back of my mind, I knew that they were escaping - not wanting to be involved in the media hounding that had begun. Already we had received several phone calls, mostly from a *Daily Mail* reporter. It would seem someone had tipped them off – maybe at the hospital, maybe a neighbour, but more likely one of Sophie's parasitic family members.

I couldn't be sure of all the reasons behind her drastic end. Her frustrations reaching a point where instead of confronting her fears, she simply refused to accept the way she was. The final act proved inconclusive: she couldn't live with herself nor have a life with me - a reminder of what she truly was. She had needed me in her life to keep herself sane, so despite our waning relationship, my presence at the very end was the ultimate insult, the ultimate kick in the teeth and the ultimate perverse way of her saying, "You failed, Nick, you failed to help me, so fuck you and deal with this instead. Let's see if you can save yourself after this." And she would be right. I felt responsible for her throughout our relationship and now felt at fault for her suicide. She had indeed fucked me up good and proper. This I would have to deal with on my own - the whole relationship, from start to finish, to be revisited again and again to fully comprehend Sophie's life and why she ended up doing what she did. If I could get all of that clear in my mind and remove every ounce of blame from myself, I might be able to move on, to banish the accusations from my head and silence her, and the voices, once and for all.

.   .   .

The car pulled off the ferry. In less than twenty minutes we would arrive at our new home. It was somewhere up a long drive, in the woods and with only one other house nearby. It sounded 'nice'. Somewhere I would have picked had my opinion counted and somewhere to get some 'me' time and think things over. For now, more than ever before, this was exactly what I needed - time to replay the relationship with Sophie over and over again in my mind to try and find hope, sense and belief in the small pockets of happiness we once shared.

There were still many things left unresolved back in the UK and my parents would have to return often to tie up all the loose ends - such was the nature of our hasty exit. I was more than happy to leave them to all the adult stuff. I wasn't sure whether they were upset about the whole Sophie incident or whether it was because they had to change their plans to move here, something they had always wanted to do, but not until retirement age. I was well aware of the burden I brought on them, not just now but from the day I was born. I was a showcase baby, something for the neighbours to see, but behind closed doors I was unwanted and a hassle. It's not that I was *unloved*, you understand, I was just a hindrance to their freedom and the lifestyle they wanted to lead. They were both journalists and were often away jostling for first coverage of various high-profile events. They worked as a team and always seemed to be the couple the celebrities wanted to work with.

Their methods of telling a story often pulled at the heartstrings of the readers and they were almost a celebrity pairing in their own right. But in reality it was all a game, a myth. They didn't give a damn about the people they interviewed, they just knew the necessary tactics - the 'ways in' to a person's mind and became 'counsellor' to all those who opened their hearts, their lives and their doors to them. They even had reporters beginning to report on them. Only a short while ago I saw photo clippings of my mother on a yacht with two brothers from a sit-com. She was topless with a champagne glass in hand, happily waving to the paparazzi taking photos of her from shore. *YouTube* even had a video of it up for a short time, before it was taken down for indecency. I had never been so embarrassed.

The life they led was unfathomable. They couldn't be any more aloof and yet people simply did not pick up on it. Even those considered closest to them were unaware of their hypocrisy - a certain a-list celebrity, cited as my Godfather, although I cannot recall ever meeting him or having any contact with him whatsoever, waxed lyrical about them. No, the work they did wasn't just to bring in the pennies. What they really sought was fame and the invites to the posh parties. Funnily enough, when my unhinged girlfriend and I provided that fame, they ran for the hills, for it were not the type of fame they desired.

When I was created, my mother wasn't strong enough to terminate me and my father was too eager to impress others. Instead, I was reluctantly brought into the world and given all the inanimate things I needed to survive. My nannies however, were always very fond of me and as I got older I was welcomed readily into friends' homes. It was as if other people knew without really knowing. Maybe it was the rigid hugs I gave or the single chair I would occupy, distanced from the rest of the household. But as I grew older and my friends became like family, the more I was able to bond and socially interact. The closeness I sought escalated at a furious pace once Sophie had come onto the scene.

.   .   .

After a short trip along the island's only dual carriageway, we meandered north, away from the coast towards woodland. It was a little after midday. The traffic, full of tourists enjoying the sun, was heading towards the beaches, but the further away from the coast, the quieter it became.

"Careful Jack!" Mum jolted out her legs.

"Don't worry, Kate, spotted," said my father calmly, as a tractor edged its way out of a field.

At any other time, he would have waved it forward, but today he glared at the farmer and gave him a wide arch as he swerved aggressively around him. I could understand my father wanting to get to the house to make my mother feel better; to make us all feel better.

I could sense his angst; my father had always tried to do the right thing where my mother was concerned. They loved each other and they loved their lives. I was left to my own devices, even from a very early age, until I had little option but to become a loner and depend on no-one. This was something I did have in common with Sophie and was one of the reasons we connected so early in our relationship. For a while we only truly had each other and it was in that short-lived time that I thought I could save her – that the two of us could take on the world with our love for one another, much as my parents had done, but the relapse was frighteningly fast, violent and tragic.

"Not far now," said my father.

My mother edged forward in her seat.

I felt physically warmer as we turned into the long gravel drive, lined by alternating horse and sweet chestnut trees. Soon they would be dispersing their fruits and shortly afterwards their leaves; a period of winter sleep would follow. I always enjoyed autumn but winter offered little to me. Christmas was supposed to be an affair for loved ones and family. I never really had the comfort of either.

You'd be lying to yourself if you believed otherwise.

The memories passed and I shivered as the car pulled in front of the new house. It was large, grey and imposing. Newly painted white sash windows looked down on me from the second floor. I felt intimidated - somewhat disconnected.

"Wow, Jack," said my mother, with more than a half smile.

"I thought you'd like it," he returned the expression and patted her knee. "Let's check it out."

Both were out of the car like a flash. Running around to the front, now hand in hand scurrying towards the house. I just sat there, alone in the back. I heard my mother giggle as both of my parents unlocked the door and bounded in. I squirmed a look away from the house and squinted across the gravel to a house opposite. How I hadn't noticed it on the way into the drive amazed me. It was again large and imposing - in fact, an exact replica of ours.

I could recall my father saying that there was one other house nearby, but I didn't expect it to be quite so close. No more than fifty yards away, maybe less. My mother, after coming off her material high would not be so enthused once she saw it and I wanted to be there when she noticed - I just had to be. Our house back home was another detached building but with no other property within a few hundred yards of us. That old thatched property was my parents' pride and joy, yet they had always dreamed of moving here at some point. To be more 'exclusive' I overheard them say once. I bit my upper lip; she was going to *love* this. It looked as if Jersey might have priced the seclusion out of their budget and I knew they would eventually blame me, for having to move before they could truly afford anything like they had at home. Still, it made me content – maybe they could re-evaluate their lifestyle now and assess what really was important. They had always believed they would move to London, New York or L.A. before finally retiring back here where they once had family.

A big fish in a small pond.

I picked at an old scar around my thumb and wiped my right eye. I always loved Jersey. My grandmother lived here her whole life and I would visit often when I was a kid. It was a place that had always been good to me and I was thankful to be in this safe-haven. I just hoped Sophie's family wouldn't come looking for me - for explanations. Her father disturbed me the most but he was weak, pathetic. After all, they knew I could blow the lid off their whole family. Sophie's secrets had become my secrets and I knew it was a risk none of them would be likely to take; surely they wouldn't be that naïve, that stupid.

I slowly edged out of the safety of the car and examined my new surroundings. To the right of our property but facing into the gravel courtyard were two large garages. Their white, rolling double doors also looked newly painted. I wondered if my father would protect the car by parking it in the garage or instead leave it out for the new neighbours to be jealous of. I smirked, already knowing the answer. Jersey was different to back home. People didn't blink an eye at posh cars, fancy watches or designer clothing. It was pretty common here. Back home my parents were affluent. Here, they were nothing special.

To the right of the garages were trees, thick and deep - a forest, no less. I could barely see daylight through it, but it looked like there might be a path. Then there was the mirror property with its own white wood sash windows, all newly painted, almost garish within its surroundings. My eyes however, were quickly drawn back towards the path - and I immediately felt my stomach turn. A young, elf-like figure with long flowing sun-kissed hair, sharp cheekbones and caramel skin, in a white summer dress and no shoes skipped amongst the trees. With each subsequent blink, the girl I had seen, melted into the darkness of the woods beyond.

CHAPTER TWO

The Path

It was daylight. I was unsure how long I had been asleep. The last thing I remember was lying on the sofa downstairs watching *YouTube Smack Cams* but failing to find them funny. My bags remained unpacked.

There had been the usual unfamiliar creaks and bumps in the house throughout the night. A door slamming and water running - which I assumed was one of my parents using the toilet. Nothing out of the ordinary. They weren't there when I awoke, but I found milk in the fridge and my favourite cereal unopened on the counter. Thank heavens for small mercies. My stomach was gurgling. I looked back in the fridge, found some orange juice, again my favourite, and diluted a pint glass half with water from the double sink in the country style kitchen. I gazed out across the courtyard at the other building whilst tearing at the breakfast box.

You missed mum's reaction.

I struggled to swallow the juice, but forced it down regardless and as I slammed the glass on the counter, the figure once again appeared, this time in the window of the house opposite. She was looking at me.

"It's not her," I said aloud. "It's *not* her." And as my eyes began to sting, the juice came back up in the sink. When I looked again, the girl was gone. I hated the fine line between what I knew was real and what I wanted to be real. I was having a hard time with that lately. I had to stop seeing her in my dreams with the screams and the blood; I just had to. Every time I closed my eyes she was there - in various states of transformation. Sometimes she appeared as angelic as on the day I first met her, whilst at other times she would appear gaunt and lifeless as in our last moment together. She would also appear in every other state in between. If this continued and stayed with me in the waking world, they'd lock me up for sure. I loved my own space and a certain amount of isolation, but not that much. I hoped that this would eventually pass and fade out; please God, it had to.

Still in my clothes from the day before, I stepped outside into the warmth of the summer. The sun was high in the sky so I assumed it must have been around midday. I surveyed what was in front of me - a property in the mirror image of our own. I wondered if both were also the same on the inside and who might live there? Thinking hard about what my idea of a perfect neighbour would entail. Thankful for my procrastination amidst the fears of dealing with Sophie; our relationship; her death.

The house, think more about the house.

I again wondered who lived there? Who *really* lived there? I also considered when my parents would be home. I needed distractions. And then I got one. A rustle of leaves and a large flock of wood pigeons flew out from the trees, heading in my direction. A slalom of thirty or more birds, all missed me by less than a metre.

The woods, there was something about the woods.

Explore. Go on. I dare you.

Trying to draw my stare away, I couldn't. I was perplexed. I wasn't sure whether this was a pleasurable experience or not? I spun around on the spot, looking upwards, blinding myself and then suddenly, she was there, again, coming out of the woods and heading towards the neighbours' house. Dark sunspots in my eyes grew smaller and I tried to call out, but what left my breath was nothing more than a whisper.

"Sophie?"

And then she was gone - through the front door of the house. I didn't know where to look, how to stand or what to do.

I took a step forward. Surely I had imagined it? Surely Sophie wasn't in there? She couldn't be? I replayed the incident in my head as my skin clung uncomfortably to my t-shirt. *Her* favourite t-shirt. I ran back inside.

Whilst rummaging through boxes, I took off my top, rubbed myself down with it and fumbled on a khaki *Converse* one - the newest I had. I was shaking. My blood raced through my veins. I knew it couldn't have been her - she had died on the floor right in front of me but yet my heart was incessant.

Dress up and dress up good, for your one true love is over the road in the house opposite, and this time everything will work out and you will save her.

I stopped fidgeting and started to sob – what the fuck was going on? Whatever I had seen couldn't have been real. Just another trick of the mind, hanging on to the coat-tails of the past, making me *want* to believe. The jitters began to relent and eventually the sobbing subsided. I gradually calmed and straightened myself but I knew that despite all of this, I had to, just had to, visit the house opposite.

I raised my hand several times in false starts to knock on the neighbours' door. Taking a deep, shudder-filled breath, I finally raised my right arm and tapped ever so lightly. I pulled myself together, adjusted my top once more and rapped the door much louder this time   then I noticed a doorbell. Grunting, I waited a few seconds and when no-one came I pressed the buzzer for a much longer period than I intended, causing me to jump back. Nothing. Not a sound from inside the house. I tried to look through the ground floor windows but both had curtains drawn. Could she have been and gone in the time it had taken for me to change? I rejected this. And then dismissed myself for ever seeing her in the first place.

How's that going? You know, your sanity?

I looked back over my left shoulder towards the trees, sighed heavily and headed to investigate.

The sun had moved to signal mid-afternoon. I had obviously lost track of time in my panic-filled quest to find a clean t-shirt and was now desperate to see what was what. I loved exploring, woods especially and as I looked upon them, I was awash with emotion.

There was always something magical about forests: the sun's rays filtering through the trees, the bird songs, the sound of running water and the stories of nymphs and fairies that sheltered under toadstools when the rain started. There were also of course, the creepy and disturbing fragments: the strange buzzing, the irregular growth of fungi causing unimaginable deformities and the storybook wolves and hobgoblins that picked off the lost. I loved that sense of wonder. I loved being able to make up stories whilst sitting in the middle of the thicket, listening to the enchanting symphony around me. I felt calmer whenever I visited the rural areas back home and now I felt that calmness here too. The thought of Sophie, still very much in my mind, receded somewhat - I had just been silly. For once, the memories that constantly smacked me in the face let up and my negativity momentarily subsided.

I was still at the opening of the path, just standing there, remembering how good things used to feel, how they *could* feel and how I wish they still felt. I blinked a couple of times and began my adventure - walking the short rise to where a path seemed to disappear.

My breathing quickened. The trail did disappear. It stopped at the very top of the slope. There was a drop of about six feet the other side but with no further man-made route to be found. It looked as if this section of the woods had been cleared for the properties to be built, and in doing so, a mound had been made with the spare earth - a private sanctuary zone for which the boundary of both properties would end here. It was a shame but at the same time it made the woods more isolated, more intriguing. Looking more intently, I could just about make out a natural path instead. It was as if it had been waiting for me.

I looked around and then by my feet for the easiest way to drop down. There were a number of roots in and around me from when they had excavated the area. It looked like every available inch of land had been used for the buildings but if so, then who owned the rest of the land and the forest beyond? I thought of farmers with blunderbusses, of *Elma Fudd* trying to gun down *Bugs Bunny* – the magic was already happening. I hoped there were fruit trees - I was always fond of wild apples. I recalled the fables I read when I was younger and believed that there was something naughty and fulfilling about stealing forbidden fruit. *Snow White* and her dwarves sprung to mind.

Eager now, I sat down and turned myself around; clambering down the largest root and at halfway I let go and dropped the final few feet. I looked back up from whence I came and cursed for not jumping down in the first place. It didn't look so high from down here; but heights and myself did not mix so well:

I had been playing in the back garden outside my childhood home with a tennis ball, throwing it against the bare brick wall of my house so that it came back to me at irregular angles. I thought it would help me to get into the cricket team - to be sharp and a good catcher. I must have been about eleven-years-old as I had just started secondary school but I was in the reserve team for everything. I hated being in the reserves and was desperate to play in the firsts. I was always jealous of how the best footballers and cricketers were given such an easy ride in school by teachers and peers alike. It was getting dark and my parents had gone out for dinner. They said they wouldn't be late.

The light from inside the kitchen illuminated the back yard just enough for me to continue playing my game. With each catch and smart piece of handling I felt closer and closer to acceptance and knew I could transfer this to the playground and finally the school field. However, as my throwing arm tired I became clumsier and I missed several catches in a row. Annoyed with myself I threw the ball haphazardly towards the wall, hitting the ledge of the kitchen window causing it to bounce up and onto the nearby shed's flat roof and into the gutter. It was the only ball I had.

I would be shouted at for losing the ball and there was no way my father, let alone my mother, would go on to the shed to retrieve it, so to save the hassle I decided to go up myself. I went inside and dragged a stepladder out from the cupboard under the stairs. I struggled but eventually set it just under the gutter. Upon climbing the ladder I was just tall enough to see onto the roof - filling me with excitement. My football was up there too - not in the gutter but right in the middle of the roof, slightly deflated. I couldn't believe my luck. I had always wondered what had happened to it.

I assessed the situation. I was too small to climb up, unless ... I looked at the ladder. There was one extra part I could stand on: the handle. Okay it wasn't officially a step, but it would make me tall enough to climb onto the roof. With both hands I clung to the gutter and stepped onto the very top of the ladder. It began to wobble, so instinctively I pushed off and pulled myself up in one swift move. I quickly spun around onto my front, but before I could grab it, the ladder toppled over and onto the yard floor. I sighed but bravado quickly took over as I avidly picked up my football and threw it down, I then grabbed the tennis ball and threw that down too. I puffed out my chest and stood tall, wishing that it was daylight so I could see more around me.

The shed roof was a fun place to be, I felt powerful up there. It was no wonder that royalty and emperors would always sit high in their thrones scanning the servants beneath them. It was the same with those at

21

the head of the lunch tables at school; it was the best footballers that always sat there. Now I had my football back, I could stop messing with the game of cricket and get back to the sport I really loved. That was where the real stars - the real leaders were made and adored. The season had already started but I knew, just knew that by practising in the yard I could be better and play with the kings in the A-team. But then I recalled my predicament. The shed roof was at least eight feet high, more than twice my size, but in the darkness, away from the kitchen light, it seemed double that. I cautiously sat on the edge of the roof, thinking about all the ways I could get down, avoiding having to jump in case I hurt myself in doing so. I thought of staying up there until my parents came home, so they could put the ladder back up and dad would come and rescue me. So I stayed there and waited.

Time passed and I was shivering uncontrollably. I was frantic. I then considered that if my parents did find me, they would not only take the football away but also the tennis ball and then I wouldn't make either first team. So I got to my feet and hunted for another way down, but as I did, I heard a car and panicked. Not even lowering myself I jumped into the darkness below and on landing there was a crack. The pain was sharp and sudden. I yelped and screamed out; retching at the way I saw my foot lay. I was in floods of tears and desperately hoped I would soon be in my parents' arms. But the car I had heard continued on its way, it hadn't been them after all.

I laid there for an hour or more, hoping that at any minute my parents would return - but nothing. Somehow I eventually pulled both myself and the ladder inside, and crawled into bed, I wasn't sure how I managed it but I had. Strangely I recall falling asleep readily yet waking up with an horrendous throbbing in my leg. It was the next day and daylight; my parents still weren't home. The last time this had happened they promised me they would never do that again and if I kept it a secret, they would get me a couple of new computer games. Of course I never said anything to anyone, even though the computer games never came. It was lunchtime before they returned, giggling as they often did after their night's out. I remembered the annoyance on their faces when they saw that I was still in bed, further still when they noticed the football in my room and then lastly at my swollen ankle.

I spent the next six weeks in plaster and finally when I was out of it, the football and tennis ball were nowhere to be seen. I never did make the first team; shortly after, I had given up playing sport altogether.

I hated that memory. It was one I hadn't thought about in a long time.

I had often spoken with Sophie about my past and my upbringing - the time when I went a whole term without a packed lunch and was given a lump sum of money instead and told to 'budget accordingly' as my parents were too busy to go shopping. I was determined to find similarities with our childhoods and the neglect we both felt. All of which fell on deaf ears but I had tried all the same. Sophie was considerate to how lonely I was but rarely interested in my past, lest of the sadness I felt; such was the overwhelming pity that she had for herself. She had after all, suffered more than any child should and her suffering was far worse than anyone else's. I had tried to understand that because whatever I went through, she had had it a thousand times worse. She kept telling me that and so in the end, I stopped confiding in her - allowing myself to be all consumed by her own traumatic upbringing. She had no time for my 'minor' issues. My parents were aloof, neglectful and dismissive. Sophie's family were a much darker proposition. In the past she had told me that they had beaten her, cut her and worse. They had done, or been party to *things* - unimaginable *things*.

I turned back towards the woods, wiping my face as I did. I blinked several times but my vision remained blurred. I jogged awkwardly into the trees, quickly finding the nearest safe-haven, away from any viewable manmade structure and sat down clumsily against a fallen log. I was thankful that I had so easily found a place of solitude where I could weep nostalgically. It was the first time I had really let myself go after the suicide - the shock finally turning to wretched desolation.

I curled into the foetal position and hugged myself to ease the shivers, despite the warm summer's day. Lying there, crying for an hour, I eventually gave in to sleep.

CHAPTER THREE

The Woods

I dreamt of Sophie. Of the days leading up to her death and just how vulnerable she was. I dreamt about the time only a few months before, where I thought I had actually got through to her. How she confessed her love for me, how she spoke about running away together and about getting out of our horrible little lives - starting afresh where no-one knew who we were:

We had just finished making love. Our legs were still entangled and I could feel the rapid beating of her heart. She was glowing, with tiny beads of sweat across her forehead and top lip. I kissed her deeply and enjoyed the salty taste.

"What are you thinking?" she asked, as I snuggled into her neck. This was a common question of hers.

"Just about us, our future, how happy I am at this moment."

"That was proper love-making wasn't it?"

"The best," I said.

"Sometimes I just love being held," she said.

"It could always be like this," I told her.

"Would you marry me, Nick? I'm not actually asking but would you?"

"Yes I would." I liked this game.

"And have children with me, you know like, we'd be proper parents and stuff?"

"If it was to always be like this I would," I replied.

"Why wouldn't it be? Go on then, what names would you call them – if we were to have one of each, I know already: Edward and Bella – proper good names." She sat up to face me with excited eyes.

I smiled wryly, "Could you be anymore mainstream?"

"I suppose you'd prefer Jacob and Alice?" she grunted.

I pulled her back down to me. "I'm happy with whatever."

I had been hopeful that this was the new Sophie. The one I always felt was inside and that all my care, attention and devotion I had shown her, was finally making her feel safe and loved. It was short-lived. For not long after, she had told me that 'I was losing her', she 'didn't know what love really was' and she 'wanted to be on her own'. The change was all too sudden. I guessed there was another person involved and when Sophie became more and more hesitant and deceitful, I doubted just how much of her I really knew or understood. She denied anything was going on and that she was just reassessing her life, but I knew, deep down, I knew. A girl like Sophie needed constant attention and when her new love interest had quickly backed out, experiencing first hand the exasperations of dating her, she had become more distraught than ever. Feeling so utterly neglected, she had tried to come back to me, but I wasn't sure about anything anymore. I still loved Sophie, but I felt exhausted with her. I didn't know what else to do so I stuck at it, trying to make her realise the causes of her actions, trying to help her but at the same time trying to keep my distance. I even managed to get her to see a counsellor. Trouble was, after one session she believed she was cured and never went again. When she had turned up on my doorstep that fateful night, soaked through and with a vacant glaze, twitching uncontrollably, I knew she had finally lost it. Minutes later, she was slitting her wrists:

Sophie was standing, facing me, chef's knife in hand.

The dream was all too real. I didn't want to go through this again, not now, not ever.

I quickly snapped out of it when something touched my face. Startled - I sat bolt upright; Sophie was in front of me.

I kicked out my legs, trying to back away. I rubbed my eyes with clammy, soiled hands.

"I'm sorry I startled you." She bowed her head, but kept eye contact.

I blinked, and then again more forcefully - trying to wash away the vision in front of me. I shook my head in disbelief, desperate to clear my mind and make sense of what was happening.

You're not my Sophie.

Eventually, as the seconds ticked away, I realised what a fool I had looked. Remembering the last moments of my dream, I felt sick. Of course it wasn't her but would I rather this girl *had* been Sophie? I really didn't know. For if it was then I would be risking insanity - again for her. And if not, then I would continue to be ...

"Are you, okay?" she asked.

My lucidity returned – it wasn't her, but someone of similar age and with that innocent, adorable quality that Sophie

29

had when we first met. My heart was beating heavily in my chest. I breathed in, greedily gulping up the forest air.

.   .   .

Everything was still. The quiet was riddled with a heavy air that threatened storms. I was hot, almost feverish. A combination of the vivid dreams; waking to face someone I thought was, wanted to be, Sophie; the humidity of the late afternoon heat.

We studied each other. I fidgeted, trying to find a comfortable posture and something to look at that would take my gaze away from the girl, without seeming rude. I found neither.

"Well aren't you going to say 'hello'?" she smiled, studying me.

I snapped out of the situation, realising just how rude I was being.

"I'm sorry," I said, "I was in a deep ... one."

"Well I'm sorry I startled you. I'm Carrie. You're my new neighbour, aren't you?"

And then it all made sense - this was the girl I had seen in the courtyard. I examined Carrie and found myself comparing her to the girl I left dying on the kitchen floor:

Carrie's features were far softer, and although they shared the same natural hair colour and were of similar age, everything about this girl seemed easier on the eye. Her mouth bore no cracked lips, but these were instead, plump and full of colour. Her skin was not pale and ashen, but flushed and smooth, and her eyes were not sunken and dark, but bright and clear. The whites of the girl's eyes were the whitest I'd ever seen, and then there was her smile. Sophie's teeth had eventually become stained by tobacco and were occasionally bloody around the gums, causing her breath to smell. This girl looked as fresh as Sophie had done when I first met her. It was how I pictured her in my mind and how I had wanted her to look.

A light breeze started up and the girl's hair fluttered, covering her face. I wanted to brush it away, but feared whom it would, or wouldn't, reveal.

"Afternoon naps are great aren't they? You've found the best spot. I come here myself sometimes," she said.

"It's not something I've done for a while," I replied, ruffling my hair. "You live in that house in the courtyard yeah?" It was the most I had said in days.

"Yes, indeed I do. You're Nick, aren't you?" Her stare was becoming intimidating.

"Yes, how did you know?" I asked.

"I heard we were having new neighbours so I did a bit of investigating. My folks aren't the best at being sociable so I knew I had to find out all about you for myself or it could have been months before I'd have known. Luckily I saw you come into the woods so I thought I'd follow you and introduce myself, but you seemed in your own little world so I tried not to disturb you."

"How long was I asleep for?" I was still coming to my senses and felt the need to continually rub my eyes.

"Oh not long, half an hour, maybe more. I was going to wake you as I heard thunder but you did that all by yourself."

"Were you just sitting there, watching me sleep?"
Rub, rub, rub.

"I know it sounds rude, but it's a really good way of getting an impression of someone." I could feel her eyes burning into me.

"And what impression did I make?" I remembered the dream and thought it could only have been negative.

"Well you didn't seem altogether happy, but I blame myself for that."

"How come?" *Now* I was being needy.

"You were obviously aware someone was here, as you seemed troubled. You flinched and then backed away when I touched ... when you woke up. Must have been a shock to have some stranger staring back at you I guess." Her guilt was sincere and refreshing. She finally broke off her stare and looked into her lap.

Touched?

My shoulders dropped. She was only looking out for me. After all, it was something I had always done for Sophie. At some point I had also stopped rubbing my eyes.

"Sorry," I said firmly. "I think it was just falling asleep in a strange place you know?"

The uncomfortable situation subsided a little. We were both well aware that these were unusual circumstances to meet for the first time. I felt somewhat exposed and Carrie had the look as if she had trespassed.

"I'm Carrie," she said again, eagerly extending out her hand this time. I thought it was ever so slightly forced, but was happy that she had decided to move the conversation on from the now mundane, disturbed sleep scenario. So I took her offering, and with that, Carrie's eyes lit up and the smile softened. I couldn't help but grin myself. Something which quickly became a chuckle. Carrie did likewise and the ice was well and truly broken.

"I'm Nick," I said, finally introducing myself even though she already knew who I was.

"Well, Nick, welcome to my woods and to Jersey," she said.

I wasn't sure which of these pointers to pick up on. Carrie saved me the hassle, "Okay, Nick *our* woods now. I guess I can share them – if you're worthy enough." Repeating her infectious expression.

I had found it very difficult in the last year to decipher exactly what people were saying to me. I was so unsure of myself that every sarcastic comment felt like a dig - when it was no such thing.

"I'm joking, Nick. I joke a lot, and that means I'll probably take the piss out of you every now and again." She studied me.

"No it's fine," I lied. "I don't mind a bit of banter."

"Really?" she questioned.

"You just remind me of someone that's all." Not a lie this time.

"Someone from back home? Where is home, Nick? Up north?"

"Yes, t'up north." I emphasised, not wanting to be any more specific.

"The north of England is lovely."

"Not where I come from."

"Oh, I'm sorry. Anyway, I'm guessing you get a lot of rain up there, so you'll feel right at home in a few seconds."

And on cue, a rumble of thunder sounded in the distance, the trees began rustling and the sky started to lose colour. The air was damp and as we both got to our feet I was aware that one side of me was much dirtier than the other.

"Home or deeper?" she asked.

I couldn't quite fathom what she was asking? I reddened slightly.

"Into the woods," she stressed.

I looked up and the raindrops started. Big, fat, heavy droplets - the type that only come in summer storms. As I looked towards home she grabbed my hand, pulling me in the opposite direction and off we went, Carrie skipping whilst I struggled to stay on my feet.

As she danced her way through the thicket, she let go of my hand and challenged me to keep up through the pouring rain and ever darkening canopy of forest, I felt my heart race. I lost sight of her one second and then saw her again the next as she fluttered in and out of the foliage. I was indeed chasing a deity through the woods and in doing so, was letting go of my inhibitions and fears thus moving faster, bringing her closer into view. But it was then that I got a little too confident - I slipped and eventually stumbled over some dead wood, falling down on my side. The thick, dense, muddy forest bottom ensured a soft landing and when I looked around for Carrie, she was thankfully out of sight. I gingerly got up and assessed the damage. I was fine, just a little dirty. A lot dirty actually. I smiled, both sides of me now matched. For a few seconds I had felt truly alive again.

I started moving once more. Walking this time, as the forest was now so dark I could barely see more than a few metres in front of me. I thought about calling out to her, but didn't want to seem pathetic, besides I was enjoying the quiet. So I carried on - on until I saw an opening in the woods and a hint of bright, alluring light. The sun had set but there was still a pink hue illuminating the sky. I followed the colour and as the path fully opened up I had to shield my eyes from the initial glare. When I was finally able to focus, I saw what the clearing presented. Despite all of the growth and the fact that most of the trees and foliage had begun to claim back their land, it was still obvious enough what it was, or rather, what it had been. I was mesmerised. Bits of broken tombstone lay fallen against each other, disturbed and unsettled. Some were stained with fading graffiti. The more I scanned the graves the more I had to squint. At the back there appeared to be a particularly big tomb, covered in moss. I felt a longing to investigate further and to attend to some of the more distressed and dishevelled plots. As I took a timid step towards the cemetery, some unseen force and a weight on my back punched my whole body forward. I reached behind me, desperately trying to throw it off. The warm air on my neck and the snarls horrified me. I was certain that I would be bitten. Spinning around with the thing on me, I sank to my knees and twisted it off onto its back. Carrie's laughter ceased as she saw the blind terror in my face peering down at her. She smiled wryly.

"Fuck, I almost..." I resisted the urge to look down at my crotch.

"Sorry, Nick, I just couldn't help it."

"I could have killed you," I said.

"Oh come on, Nick did you not hear me whispering in your ear."

"Whispers? Jesus, they were like horrible little snorts." I turned my back on her, and this time I did check myself, all ok thankfully. Running my fingers through my hair and with the panic over, I managed a little snort of my own.

I looked back at her. She was still sitting there, her eyes looking up at me, her head bowed slightly.

"I was trying to whisper to you but I was a bit out of puff," she said.

I looked behind her towards the cemetery.

"What is it?" she asked, looking in the same direction.

"I just stumbled onto something; someplace." I said, and immediately wished I hadn't.

"Really? Shit, I hadn't realised we had come this far."

I studied her as she turned back towards me.

"The cemetery, huh?" she asked nonchalantly.

"You've been here before then?"

"To be honest, I tend not to come this far - well in this direction I mean. There's a lake nearby and I usually go there. Well I say lake, I guess it's really a pond. We don't have any lakes in Jersey. *Pool* is probably a more appropriate word, and far more grand than pond don't you think?" She didn't wait for an answer. "And there's also a disused little house the other way, but that's quite a bit further down the cliff path to the sea. It has some cool history." She walked quickly up to me, grabbed my hand and began to lead me away.

"C'mon, Nick, I'd better get you home."

As we hastily walked back through the forest I desperately tried to remember the way. I wanted to come here again tomorrow and check out the cemetery I had just stumbled upon. When I mentioned it to Carrie, she said she'd rather go to the pool or to the run down cottage and show me the sea. I was tempted by both but also knew I still had two weeks to go until the start of school, so was in no immediate rush.

"Ok I'll take you to the cemetery, but after I've shown you the pool and cottage, deal? It will be a let down though, I can promise you that. Apparently the place hasn't been used for years which is why it's such a mess."

"Why is that do you think?" I asked.

"I'm not that interested to be honest but I'll ask my dad tonight, he might have an idea. See you tomorrow, Nick, you know the way from here." And with that, she rushed off towards the rise, nimbly climbing the exposed roots and up onto the path. Then she was gone - out of sight.

Cautiously, I also climbed up - not realising we had already passed where we first met. I stumbled slightly and wiped the sweat from me. Wearily I got back onto the track and saw the lights on in Carrie's house. These helped to guide me the rest of the way, across the courtyard, back to my own place. In my room, all of my belongings were now out - in a perfect replica of my room back home. I felt a lump in my throat. My parents had duplicated the safe solitude we used to have in our old house - one of the only places I had felt safe recently, other than the woods. My bed was freshly made with clean and familiar sheets; white underlay with a pale blue cover on a summer duvet. My pillows were in matching pale blue cases and neatly placed at the head of a small double bed. They had even put up the signed poster of my favourite band I got off *eBay* on the wall opposite the window. I stripped off to my boxer shorts and lay on the bed. Despite the stifling heat, I was asleep in seconds.

CHAPTER FOUR
The Pool

The following morning I again woke to an empty house. The move hadn't seemed to bring us closer as yet, but I had belief — one of my good traits, but one that often erred on being ever so slightly gullible. I wanted to believe the best in people and take them at face value. But I also knew that this wasn't always the case and in recent times I had become far more sceptical. I found this a hard concept to fathom - my dream of a fairy tale existence, which kept finding disappointment at every turn, yet none of it seemed to be my fault. Was the way I went about my everyday life, the way in which I treated people, or offered myself totally, such a poor persona of oneself? On stage and open armed - only to be knocked down.

I was annoyed with how I had been with Carrie the previous day - how I enjoyed her company and yet was so off with her. The barriers were definitely up and I needed to find a way, and fast, to bring them down between us or I would miss the opportunity to make my first friend in Jersey. The way yesterday had ended was testament to the issues I now had in meeting new people, especially someone as beautiful and receptive as Carrie. Everything she did I both loved and hated at the same time. The way she floated about, playing silly games. The way she spoke with such energy and excitement about the world around her - all too familiar - for it was also the way I used to feel about life. Even with my aloof parents, I still felt energised and determined enough to make some truly great friends. I knew girls who had liked me but I had waited. I always believed that one day the girl who was meant to be, would walk right up to me, somewhere where I'd least expect it and that we would fall passionately in love. I then remembered the first time I had met Sophie.

My stomach somersaulted. I took a deep breath and closed my eyes. I wanted to hate Sophie. As much as I disliked the terrible and disturbing memories, I preferred them to the beautiful heart-wrenching ones.

I felt sick, so instead of breakfast I poured a glass of water. At the kitchen window I looked across the courtyard towards Carrie's house, watching avidly for any sign of life. We hadn't arranged a time to meet. I wasn't even sure if we would meet, such was Carrie's hasty departure yesterday. So if she didn't come out soon to call for me, I would just go on my own. As much as I enjoyed my own company, now more so than ever, having Carrie around gave me something else to think about and for that I was grateful.

I decided to head out anyway. I remembered that I hadn't yet looked into the garage that was to the left of the property as I came out of the front door. It was a double garage, two of them in fact. One belonged to our house and the other to Carrie's. Neither had any cars parked in front, but there were tyre tracks from what looked like two cars parked end-to-end in front of the one owned by my parents. I hadn't heard any vehicles in the night and couldn't recall if the neighbours' car had been there when I came through the courtyard yesterday. If I had a mobile I would text one of them - my dad probably, to say thank you for sorting out the room, but in the last couple of months of Sophie's life she had taken mine to replace hers:

My parents were away that weekend and we had the place to ourselves. We had spent the day talking about the need for her to see a counsellor and she readily agreed. She had seemed more positive and upbeat as the day wore on and although she still denied any involvement with another boy, I believed it was just a matter of time before she broke down and confided in me. I hoped that because of her agreement to see a professional, this was a step in the right direction for us.

Sophie had been in the bath while her phone was on charge in the kitchen. I was boiling the kettle to make a cup of tea and her phone quietly beeped to signal a message had come through. Usually I would ignore it - it was her phone, her message. But considering our situation lately and the fact that she still vehemently denied any wrongdoing, I just had to check this one time. As I went to pick it up I could hear the sloshing of bath water.

"Was that my phone?" she called.

I looked at the phone; the message was from someone called D:

Please stop sexting me, if you carry on I will ...

And before I could read the rest I caught Sophie out of the corner of my eye. She hadn't even bothered to grab a towel and lunged at me for the phone.

"How dare you, you fucking arsehole," she screamed. "That's private!"

I slid away from her, making her clutch at thin air.

"Who's D?" I asked.

"It's someone hassling me, give it back. Stop being a wanker!"

"Well let me read it then and I can sort it."

44

"It's personal for fucks sake!" And then she slapped me, hard across the face. *"If you ever want this again you bastard,"* pointing down at her herself, *"then give it to me!"*

I then did something rather haphazardly; I opened the kettle and dropped the phone in.

I'm not sure whether the screams were louder before, during, or after she put her right hand in to retrieve it.

.   .   .

I tried to turn the metal, cigar-shaped handle of the garage door from its vertical position, but it wouldn't budge. There was a keyhole in the centre of the lever so I went back inside to see if a key was hanging up in the kitchen. In our old house, all the keys had their own hooks on a corkboard next to the kitchen door. However my mother still went through a daily ritual of hunting for keys in every handbag each morning, while the corkboard hooks stayed vacant. So it was no surprise that in our new kitchen, I found a set of empty key hooks. I would just have to wait until their return, whenever that might be.

A knock at the door brought my mind sharply back to the present. I took a quick breath and opened it to an excitable Carrie.

"Ready to go?" She was bouncing on the spot.

I needn't have worried.

"Yes definitely. The cemetery, yeah?"

Carrie pulled a face. "Not today, Nick, there's far more exciting places than that miserable old cemetery. I want to show you the pool - look I have a picnic." Carrie twisted to show the backpack she was wearing. There was a small yellow and green 'peace badge' attached to it. Sophie had had one exactly the same pinned to her denim jacket. I hurried her out of the doorway and across the courtyard towards the woods.

The pool was obviously Carrie's favourite place by the way she lit up whenever she spoke of it. The little old house I assumed would be our second port of call and the cemetery, well, that would just have to wait a day or so. Like she said yesterday, we had plenty of time to explore - and plenty of time to get to know each other. Both of which intrigued me equally.

As we entered the woods, the late morning sun on our backs became intermittent. The air felt crisper than the previous day and the woods much brighter for it. The forest was awash with a million shades of green and the smell was intoxicating. Everything seemed more detailed as if in high definition. My first decent night's sleep since the tragedy had truly been a godsend. I could now really begin to appreciate what was right on my doorstep. Whilst Carrie stopped to adjust a shoelace on her *Vans* trainers, I simply closed my eyes and sucked in the air.

We eventually arrived at where the path split into three. It had taken us much longer to reach this far into the woods than yesterday. Carrie had walked at a casual pace to allow me to take in the surroundings. She wanted me to become familiar with the area so if we ever became separated, I would know which way to return home.

"Okay, Nick, left or right?" she asked.

"Well I guess we're not going straight on?"

"No, Nick, that's not a path well trodden. I know you really want to visit the cemetery but I dislike the place. I'll fill you in on what my father said about it later, but for today I'm going to show you one of our more glamorous surroundings. Besides, it's *my* day today, so beach or pool?"

"I didn't think I had a choice?"

Carrie giggled. "Nope, I just wanted you to guess which way the pool was."

"It's right, Carrie. I'm not that clueless." I dumbed down my voice as best I could.

"Well done, fellow explorer," she was doing a little jig. "You'll love it, Nick, you really will. If you're anything like me that is."

"Hmm, bonkers crazy," I muttered.

"Yes, exactly that."

But instantly I queried my own comment. I was pleased she had taken it so lightly and didn't reference it back to myself, but I was also pleased that I was finding some kind of humour in which to personally mock myself - girls liked that. Even so, I was still slightly disturbed by how callous my comment had been - considering what I was going through. I tried not to beat myself up about it, yet my insecurity continued to linger.

The trail to the pool immediately descended as we left the main path. A trickle of water appeared out of a small cluster of rocks embedded on the right-hand-side. The stream increasing with every few steps until it became, "Wahoo a babbling brook!" I exclaimed. Carrie giggled at my delight. I looked up at her and smiled.

"This fills the pool." Carrie had a habit of answering my unasked questions.

"Must have been happening for some time to create this?" I said.

"It's not always here. Most of the time in summer the stream isn't here at all. The storm last night has probably created this for you. Good timing huh?"

"I guess so," I shrugged.

"This is why it was so important to come today - after a night of rain, the flow usually peaks around lunchtime and it's just the very best time to swim in it. The water is much warmer as it trickles over the summer soil and it's pretty much the only time you get the full benefit."

Ok, now I really was intrigued. Carrie was talking in riddles, speaking faster and faster, "We're here at the most perfect time," she purred.

We continued to zigzag, following the contours created by the water. I rushed on, desperate now to see the pool when Carrie suddenly screamed at me, "Stop, Nick, stop!" She grabbed my backpack, pulling me sharply down with her.

Small rocks kicked up in front of us and disappeared. We were at a ridge, deceptively hidden by the foliage.

"You ok, Nick?"

"Yeah fine." I blew out my cheeks.

"You have to be careful around here."

Was she mocking me?

"What? Just like you were last night? Dancing around the place." I nudged her.

"I've been here like forever, Nick, I know the area. Besides, it's only when you get off the main path that things become a little dangerous. Come, you're going to love this." Carrie got to her feet and held out her hand for me. She was beaming. I avidly got up and let her lead me, cautiously, to the edge of the ridge.

"Whoa," I said, stumbling back.

"Pretty impressive huh? Although it's much higher on the other side."

I slowly approached the edge once more, allowing the stream to flow between my feet. Now more prepared, I watched the water fall over the ledge into a crystal pool ten feet below. Three steep, granite sides imposed themselves around it, the tallest of those were opposite us and at almost four times higher than where we were currently standing. To our right was a muddy area with a grassy verge. The left-hand-side of the pool, the back, was the darkest but also the most serene. Without the sound of the smallest cascades from between my feet, the pool would be deathly silent. I was instantly in love with the place. All thoughts of wishing to visit the cemetery were now a million miles away.

I squeezed Carrie's hand and she acknowledged the compliment. "It's at its most peaceful in the summer. There's less rainfall and so the waterfalls aren't so big."

"Waterfalls?"

"Yes, there are two. The one you're interrupting ... " Carrie pointed down at my feet. " ... and there's one that comes out towards the top of the rock opposite. It's pretty amazing when that one really gets going but in summer you need a storm, a really big one to see that, but you also need light and full moon is best. Of course to get the two around the same time together is pretty uncommon. If we have a storm during the day then I rush out here to see it by moonlight. It's always at its best then. I came here last night but the rain didn't ease up and I couldn't see a thing."

I instantly put my hands in my pocket and kicked out at a small rock beside me, kicking it into the pool.

51

"It's a pity you weren't in when I knocked," she said, taking me by surprise.

"But I was in," I told her. "I must have been out for the count."

"Well I'm pleased I didn't wake you twice in one day and like I said, it wasn't worth it anyway."

I wished she had done all the same.

"So, how do we get down?" I asked.

"We jump," she informed.

I looked at her. A nervous smile crept out. I gave her the eyebrows and she grinned back.

"Ok maybe not today, seeing at it's your first time and your wobbly legs look unlikely to play ball."

She sympathetically grabbed me by the hand, leading me through no obvious route amongst some trees to our right.

"Maybe I should just have let you run straight out, Nick, what an incredible feeling that would have been huh?"

"Oh yeah, me shitting my pants as I fall off the edge."

"Ha-ha, I'm sure it would have been more divine than that, Nick, a proper soul cleanser I reckon. The most romantic of scenes."

I felt that she must know something. When she disturbed my sleep yesterday she had said I had seemed 'troubled'. I wondered how long it would be before she started asking questions. Questions I didn't feel ready to answer and answers I didn't want examining - by myself, let alone anyone else.

"Maybe next time," I said without any conviction. But it was the emotion I felt when I saw the pool that made me all the more unsteady. It was like some place I'd always dreamed about visiting, on travels around the world with Sophie. I had seen water cascading into exotic lakes on the television and couples, all alone, making love in these, the most idyllic of places and now Carrie was talking about the romance of the place and I could feel it. My legs *had* been wobbly, but that was because I *had* wanted to jump. My heart had wanted me to jump, to wash away all of the pain I felt inside. If Carrie hadn't caught me in time then what? Would I have been cleansed? I would never know the answer.

The route criss-crossed and descended steeply. Carrie made light work of the challenge whilst I grabbed trees to steady myself. Soon enough, the path levelled and through a myriad of tall, tightly knit shrubbery and opened out to a small patch of sun-kissed grass, leading up to the water's edge. I could hear the waterfall whisper its attendance in this otherwise still oasis. I was in awe.

From below, the cliffs around me showed no woodland, just sheer granite with a pinkish hue on each side. The base of the furthest was in total darkness. I squinted to try and make out the bottom of the cliff and the back of the pool, but could not.

"It's a cave, Nick. Our very own cave!" Carrie told me, "I've always been a bit too chicken to investigate for long but now you're here ... "

"Just like the cemetery." I nudged her.

"No, Nick, not like the cemetery," she grimaced.

"I'm only messing," I tried to reassure her.

"I'm not the one who needs to make friends remember - I can get along fine on my own," she said.

I was gutted. She had bitten, albeit however small, she made her point clearly and concisely. I had no place to hide.

"You're right. And I am sorry, it's just ... " Right there and then I wanted to open up and explain everything; the whole reason I was here and why I was in such turmoil. If she had only known me a few years ago.

"In your own time, Nick," she begun, "but that time had better not be too far off, or we shall both suffer."

I glanced at her, my brow raised.

"I do like having company, but if it's bad company, then I'd rather not," she finished.

This struck a chord with me. I always believed experiences were best shared - but now knew that even the best experiences, with the wrong person, could make them so insignificant, shallow and at the utmost, disheartening. I had grown to realise that these utopian experiences with Sophie had only been in my head. This pool could have been so much different, it could have been the place where I found that sanctuary I'd read about and seen on travel sites - and shared it with my new friend, but instead I found myself wishing that Sophie had been with me instead. For her to see somewhere like this and for me to be the one she experienced that with, would have surely made her open her eyes to what could truly happen if you really believed in the world, and in ourselves, as a couple. I fought to stifle the memories of when I had taken her to similar places of great expectation and tranquillity - those I thought at this very moment, were not a patch on what this place could have done for her, or for us.

There was a well-known hang out called 'LovEscape' a few miles away from where I lived. I knew a few people who had got lucky for the first time up there. I had been dating Sophie for a couple of months and was aware that the place offered great views over the city. Although unable to drive, there was a hotel further up on private land which was supposed to be the best in the area. I always thought the place to be a bit tacky anyway, and besides, I had already lost my virginity to Sophie on our first date, so the full 'iconic' potential of LovEscape was always going to have passed me by.

Sophie thought it would be fun to 'pinch' her dad's car and drive up there. I told her I had something better in mind and we wouldn't need the car. This excited her.

It was just into the New Year and the snow had been falling heavily all day. I was worried that my plan was going to go one of two ways. That it would fail dramatically or that it would be perfect – both due to the snowfall. We had made the necessary arrangements with our parents that we were staying out at 'other' friends' overnight and I met Sophie at the end of our street and walked with her to the church. Sophie was getting more and more desperate to know what was going on. Her curiosity turning once again into a very public sexual desire. She was all over me and thankfully the taxi I had ordered arrived promptly, or I think we would have done it there and then in the churchyard.

She looked at me doe-eyed as she climbed in and began fidgeting with herself the nearer we got to LovEscape, yet stiffened as we drove straight past.

"You're worth more than a quickie on LovEscape," I confided, but her head stayed transfixed towards the place as we passed. "The hotel has much better views and we'll get some privacy," I blurted out.

On arriving at the hotel, she was quiet, rejecting my attempt to hold hands. But as I mumbled through the check-in process, something I had never done before, she whispered loudly in my ear, "This is actually quite naughty, Nick, I like it."

I grabbed our bags and rushed past the waiting bellboy to our tiny room that was on the ground floor. I was inside her before we even got to the bed.

Afterwards, I sat at the window and motioned Sophie over. Pulling the duvet around us, we entwined as the sun set, beyond the car park, over the town to a gorgeous plethora of reds only found in a winter sky.

I squeezed her tightly, feeling the closest I had ever done with her. We were like a real couple now, making love in the most romantic of places near our home town that was embraced with a fairy tale covering of snow.

Sophie broke off and eased away from me, "You could have gotten us a better room," she muttered as she stood up and returned to bed, before turning her back and going to sleep.

"Sorry for seeming so unappreciative, Carrie." I started. "It really is an awesome sight and I am happy to be here. It just got to me that's all. You know ... memories." I was reluctant to say anything but felt she deserved some kind of explanation.

"Well then, let's get in the water and see if we can wash away some of that tension," she flashed a smile.

I didn't want to. I felt naked enough already without stripping down into my swimming shorts, yet Carrie was already changing - having the foresight to put a bikini on underneath. I really needed to make the effort. I had moped enough already and was concerned that Carrie would soon grow tiresome of my opposing attitude. I know I certainly was.

I turned my back on her, wishing I could hide. Fumbling with my rucksack I got out a beach towel and unrolled it, causing my shorts to fall out onto the grass. I wrapped the towel around myself and clumsily got changed, making every effort to keep myself covered at all costs. I edged off my t-shirt and folded my arms, awaiting Carrie's derogative comments, yet none came. I spun around and she grinned, before heading towards the water and sauntering in. I looked away only momentarily – other than with Sophie, I had no experience of being close to semi-clad girls and never in broad daylight with the sun burning overhead. She was a sight to behold. Her small slender body, now relieved of her hippy jeans, flowery dress and geeky rucksack, simply shone. Her skin without a single visible blemish was taught, smooth and tanned. I noticed a festival band on her left wrist as she teased the bikini bottom out from her and entered the water.

I quickly followed in behind. The crystal clear water - a refreshing relief from the muggy air. I was thankful for the numbness it caused and once past my waist I sunk into the depths, all the way under before easing myself forward, fully submerged. The weightlessness was a blessing. I opened my eyes to blearily make out Carrie's red and white bikini slightly above me and paused to watch her swim further away. I lifted myself off the bottom of the pool, causing a dust cloud and on reaching the surface, inhaled deeply. It felt good. The warm air filled my lungs as I squinted to see Carrie disappear into the shaded, imposing part of the pool.

"Come, Nick, I've something for you to experience," she encouraged.

I was uneasy about following her into the unknown, but as always, she was making me curious.

I swam, keeping my head high above the water to try to see where I was going. Yet this only prolonged the dread.

She called out to me again, "Just a bit further, Nick."

59

Cautiously, I entered the darkness.

Once entombed I stopped but I could still hear her, telling to me to come ever deeper. I treaded water and shivered, the air was much cooler here. My eyes slowly began to adjust and I could just about make her out in the distance at what seemed like the entrance to a cave. I became spooked and felt an urge for company so I picked up the pace and propelled into front crawl, determined though to still keep my head out of the water and fixated on Carrie. But as I got closer, her appearance became muddled and disfigured. My eyes became sore and sensitive - I could taste salt. Too late to turn back I splashed forward in a panic and quickly came up to where she was. She turned to face me. My eyes fought with what I was seeing. The stinging sensation made them stream and Carrie looked deathly pale, her blonde hair now matted and dark against her head; she looked like Sophie the last time I saw her. I backed off, pushing at the water in between us and rubbed my eyes again.

"Warm huh?" she said despondently.

I blinked hard and my eyes cleared. She was smiling an accomplished grin and I felt instant relief. She looked pale, sure, but she *was* in near darkness. The water, oil-like, glimmered, making strange shapes, which glistened, all around the cave. It was as if God had turned on aurora borealis just for us. I hung there, looking all around me.

"It's incredible," I said. All fears now dormant.

"The temperature or the cave?" she asked, her eyes alive.

I hadn't noticed the sudden change in the water. The air inside the cave was certainly much cooler but the water was definitely ... warm.

"What ... ?" I stopped shivering.

"Must be hot springs or something - it's salty too. Maybe even a nuclear power outlet or something," she continued in fast tongue, "but I've been coming here for years and it hasn't affected me." She twisted her face and then smiled.

But in that brief moment, I saw Sophie again.

"Please, no more faces ok, at least not in here," I pleaded.

She studied me and whilst judging my stare she whispered, "This place can help rid you of those ghosts, Nick. I can help rid you."

I was taken aback. I didn't want to talk to anyone, lest with the girl who was taking me away from the horrors of those memories and who helped dampen the voices. But now they were shouting at me again - commanding me to talk, to announce just what had happened to me over the last two years and just how close I'd come on a daily basis since then, in joining Sophie.

"If you can't talk to me, then you'd better talk to someone. You can't handle this grief on your own, it's obvious."

And now it was time for me to twist my face into a scowl. She knew I didn't have anyone to talk to. I didn't want this, whatever we had, to be a part of the healing process, a way of helping me forget; understand; accept Sophie and my relationship with her. Yet at the very heart of all this, I knew Carrie was right. I couldn't deal with it; I needed help - her help.

My face softened. I took a breath and went to say something but instead, allowed tears of a new kind, to flow without restriction. She approached me instantly, sympathetically and without reserve. Her actions were heartfelt, honest and with an integrity that I had never before experienced. She carefully placed her arms around my neck and latched onto me. I stiffened, but in realising she wasn't going to let go, my shoulders relaxed and I hugged her delicately back. Her skin, supple under my hands and warm against my chest was a welcome blessing of absolute comfort. I sobbed. The outpouring was brief but intense. I went limp in her arms and she held me until I felt ready to let go.

"Thanks," I said, "I didn't realise how much I needed that."

"Pleasure, Nick," she replied, both of us were trying to avoid eye contact.

"So how long have you been coming here?" My voice, timid.

"For as long as I can remember. Well, for as long as I was able to explore the woods on my own. It freaks me out a little, so I never stay for too long, but now you're here I find it an altogether more ... enlightening experience."

"So no-one else knows about this place?"

"It's private land, I think."

"So you've not been here with anyone else?" I finally asked the question I'd been wanting to since arriving at the pool.

"Nope, consider yourself most privileged!" she replied. And I did. For the first time, I felt myself glow, and not through embarrassment. I considered myself, in that very moment, to have been so lucky to have moved here, to have found a new friend in Carrie and to have been invited to this place. I had however, felt lucky when I first met Sophie, the girl who deceitfully wanted to experience everything with me for the first time. I thought again, that if there was a way of eradicating the previous two years I would take it, but then my mind wandered too freely and I thought too long about Sophie and felt ashamed for wanting those years gone.

"You had enough?" Carrie asked.

I nodded.

"It's quite overwhelming and a lot to take in. Come, I'll race you back and we can dry off on the grass." Carrie sped off and I took a final moment to look around. On my own the place was too quiet. The echoes no longer sounded and the cave seemed claustrophobic. I understood that it was a place for short visits, spiritual visits. I remembered that I was once like Carrie. I was inquisitive: the explorer type, happy to go anywhere, chat to anyone and to always ask the question: *What if?* The unknown used to excite me, but now it unsettled me - much in the way that every time I met up with Sophie, the initial few minutes would be testing - I would have to gauge her mood and work it from there. A little while into the relationship and it wasn't just her mood I would have to gauge - it was her appearance; her demeanour; her obscurity; her secrecy.

Carrie was already wading out of the water. I was caught staring as she turned around, yet was beamed another winning smile and motioned to come join her. I hurriedly swam forward into the cooler, salt-free water and on reaching the bank, finally dragged myself out. It had been an incredible experience. The pool had revitalised certain dormant feelings within me; some good, some bad and I had finally cracked in front of Carrie and realised that it hadn't been such a bad thing.

I appreciated the sun on my body as I left the water. Seeing Carrie's eyes on me, I quickly joined her on the picnic blanket she had laid. I reached for my towel and dabbed at my skin before using it to rest my head on, then turning over to mimic Carrie's posture.

"I can't believe how amazing this place is," I said.

"We're lucky huh?"

"Yes, I guess we are." I summed up my thoughts, trying to put everything in perspective.

Carrie reached over and ruffled my hair.

"What?" I said, looking perturbed.

"Your positivity is infectious," she said.

"Well I..."

"I know, Nick, you can't be too happy huh? It's not the right time." And that was true. At any other time I would have been deliriously happy. I was lying on a warm grassy verge next to a pool of ever-changing colours, alongside someone who was painstakingly beautiful in every way imaginable - this was the dream, my dream. Yet every time I smiled or felt a tinge of happiness I remembered Sophie, the love I had, still had for her, and an overwhelming guilt that she was not, could not, be here, to share it with me instead.

"Stop fighting it," she said. "Allow yourself to enjoy the happy feelings. You can't stay like this forever."

"You don't understand," I whispered. "No one does."

"You think you're the only one in the world who's had a shitty relationship?"

"There can't be too many that turned out like mine though."

"I'm sorry, Nick, truly I am, but you have to let her go. Stop punishing yourself for it."

I looked at her, frowning. Did she really know what had happened? Had mum and dad spilt the beans? Had it been so obviously etched on my face that it showed not just of loss, but also of complete and utter torment? But then of course, it would have been on the news, on the Internet, on *Facebook*,

MySpace and *Twitter*: '*Family Flees Suicide Scene!* With pictures posted up of the blood smeared kitchen where I last held her – with comments underneath from people I didn't know, accusing me of not helping enough and why I didn't see it coming. I wanted to ask Carrie outright, find out for sure what she knew.

Before I had time to quiz her, she caught me off guard.

"What was she like the first time you met her?"

And before I knew it ... I was simply answering.

"Sophie, her name was Sophie." I surprised myself - keen to share a little of my old life.

Carrie dug around in her rucksack and pulled out two French-sticks wrapped in cling-film. I could see the salad spilling out of the sides. She handed me one, along with a carton of juice. It felt rehearsed, as if she was trying to make me feel as comfortable as possible, but the thing was, it was working, and I was ready.

"Go on," she said.

CHAPTER FIVE

Her

I sighed deeply and thought of our first ever meeting, more than two years earlier. My heart ached, my stomach knotted and I took a couple of very shallow breaths.

"I remember it was around the time when my mother came home all excited with a signed copy of the last book in the Twilight series; not the author's signature, but Kristen Stewart's. I thanked her but when she immediately asked to borrow it, I knew I wouldn't see it again. That night, across from her at the dinner table, I re-read Bram Stoker's Dracula.

I needed to get away from them even though I craved their company. I was desperate to find some affection. A few of my friends often went clubbing and spoke about how much fun they'd had. Having never been myself, I guess you would say I was a little 'green' and which is possibly why I became so star-struck when for once, I joined them.

It was the end of the school year and there was to be a big get together before we all moved into our final year of GCSEs. The two schools in the area: Sage Green Grammar School, which I attended and Wakehouse Comprehensive, the shittier of the two, had planned a huge party for a way to socially connect with one another.

There had been incidents between the two schools all year, usually to do with each other's football team, and a few random wannabe meatheads had jumped on the bandwagon. Things had become pretty bad and a lad from our school spent some time in hospital after a firework was thrown and exploded in his face. Ever since then, the education authorities had been trying to think of ways to amend ties: organise fundraisers, you know, that sort of thing.

I hung out with a few of the football lads and although I didn't play anymore, I could talk a good game. They were all well excited about the party - some, because it was a chance for a bit of a scrap, whilst for the others it was just the excitable anticipation about seeing a whole load of new girls their age in a neutral venue. One lad, John, who I was really good friends with, was determined that I should come along as he knew of some real stunners from Wakehouse." I stopped musing, quickly reversing my smirk before Carrie motioned for me to continue.

"John, well he spoke with such animation that I eventually agreed to go, just to see him in action. I was also after some tips as girls were a bit of a foreign object to me. I was fine with my friends and teachers and could even stick up for myself if needed but if there was a girl in school who I kind of liked then I was ... well ... hopeless. I would just feel myself blushing and unable to put two coherent words together. I'd always mumble an excuse and get out of the situation but then feel a right twat afterwards." Carrie was now stifling her own grin.

"So anyway, we went to the party and it started off pretty quiet. The teachers had employed security just in case and those that had gotten smashed beforehand weren't allowed in. I had met John, along with a couple of other lads, Stuart and Adrian I think, at the pub where John's dad worked and we had a pint each, along with some chips. John had also bought a 2-litre bottle of cheap cider at the local off-license to drink on the way and we shared this between us. I wasn't much of a drinker and was therefore quite ticking by the time we arrived."

The party was full of people. Many of which I didn't know or recognise until I could see them much closer up. Girls from our school looked so different: loads of make-up and bizarre hairstyles - trying to look like Katy Perry with pink hair and tight dresses. Same with the guys too - although most of them looked better than the girls. The current craze in tattoos and piercings was certainly pro testosterone.

John was doing circles of the hall, stopping to speak to anyone who would listen. I clung by him - nodding in all the right places and laughing on cue but I loved it: the buzz, the music, the flirting. I lost track of the amount of girls who purposely brushed past me. Even though I didn't fancy any of them I was getting attention - masses of it and it felt good. None of them though were that special - yet all of that changed when she walked into the room.

We were standing by the doors when I noticed John's demeanour shift. Over my shoulder he had spotted someone. Her hair: long, neat, blonde and straight was tucked behind pixie ears showing off a tanned face and large, brilliant white, teeth. She fiddled with a pale blue, festival bracelet she had on her left wrist before advancing forward.

Everything became enlightened - spiritual almost. All of my senses heightened and seemed to tune into her. She was close enough for me to see every contour in her face and smell the exquisiteness within. I could taste her delicate beauty in the air. I desperately wanted to hold her - hold her close, for our souls to bind and become as one. I was infatuated. The way she held herself, the way she floated into the room — she didn't just walk in, she glided. Her red, strapless dress, which tied at the back in black ribbon, similar to a bodice, fluttered as she confidently started to interact with the party. She was full of smiles, her large doe-like green eyes darting on everyone and everything. She waltzed through wave after wave of cheek-to-cheek kisses before hugging John. He knew her — I was both shocked and delighted. But while she hugged him her eyes looked deeply into mine and simply sparkled. Her smile was instant and infectious. My knees buckled ever so slightly, and as she pulled away from John, she whispered something to him whilst keeping her gaze to mine.

"This is Nick," John started, "he's a great lad."

Slightly put on the spot and taken aback by his kind words, I managed to mouth out the word, "Hi."

"Hi, Nick, lovely to meet you. You're not leaving are you?" Dreamlike.

"Err, no. Not at all. John was just looking for someone."

"It would appear he found her."

John was in the clutches of a tall, dark-haired girl in a blue satin dress. That was all I could make out.

"Well I'm glad you're staying, I'm going to be here 'til the death." And with that, she spun off, grabbing the girl in the blue dress and taking her with her.

John was left in mid-air. His puzzled face turned to me. He scratched his head and then burst out laughing.

"Yes! Now that's why we came here. I knew, just knew it, that she would come. She'd never want to miss out," he said.

"Who, who was that?" I asked

"That was Claire, I've fancied her for years – we used to go to nursery and primary together and our mum's are good friends. I was gutted when I ended up at Sage Green with her at Wakehouse," he laughed. "We need to double date."

*"Wait, hang on a sec, you have to tell me - just who was **that** girl?" I begged.*

"I knew you'd like her mate – she's a proper party girl and good fun, actually looks better than I remember. I only know her, as she's a friend of Claire's. She was always encouraging me to try it on with her – Claire I mean. I just wish she hadn't pulled me off her – I need to keep my hands in my pockets now." His cheeky-chappy grin increasingly becoming a pant.

"So what's her name?" I was getting desperate.

"Sophie. Sophie Pemberton."

And there you have it. Sophie Pemberton came into my life that day. And a little over two years later she left my life and this world (I didn't tell Carrie that part). I still wasn't sure whether or what she knew, but I was becoming more and more convinced that she didn't actually know how it all ended. One day I would tell her, but she needed to know much, much more before that happened. She had to understand Sophie, understand our relationship, and realise just how quickly things became so fucked up. The first date with Sophie was a prerequisite for what was to follow. I should have backed out then. I knew, the minute she told me her darkest secret, that I should have run a mile. The call for help; her troubled past; her lack of any true emotion should have sent alarm bells crashing in my skull. But instead, and by the second date, I believed I was meant to save her. I believed I had found the fairy tale.

.   .   .

"Those friends you speak of, did you fall out with them?" Carrie waited for an answer but seeing that I was struggling she continued, "It's just that you mention them so fondly when you talk about the past that I thought they might have been there for you when everything went bad? I'm just struggling with the whole concept of your family coming out here." It was clear that Carrie didn't know what had happened after all.

"I never really spoke to them about her," I replied. "They knew of her, like I said, and we all started to hang out together but she preferred it to be just the two of us. Whenever I said about meeting up with the others or having people over, she would make out that I didn't enjoy her company and hers alone. She also said that a couple of my friends had tried it on with her once when she bumped into them when they were out and that I shouldn't trust them."

"And how did you react to that?" she asked.

"I stopped seeing them. I felt it strange that they would even bother calling me up considering they did what they did."

"So you didn't actually confront them?"

"I was going to. I was due to meet them to watch the football one day and then Sophie told me in more detail what had happened. I said I would have it out with them but she pleaded with me not to. She said they were very drunk and probably wouldn't remember it and the best thing I could do was just ignore them. Pretty soon, I stopped hearing from them altogether."

"And what do you think now?"

"That it doesn't make sense. Sophie was always critical of their laddish ways but they all had girlfriends and were always respectful of that fact. Why would they pick her of all people to mess around with, unless it was to get at me?"

"Or unless she wanted to get at you," Carrie interrupted. "Unlike with you Nick, she's not making a very good first impression on me."

"Well you've kind of cut to the chase already."

"I'm only saying how I see it. Did it not occur to you at the time that she might have made that story up, or even worse - have tried it on with your friends?"

"Not at the time. But she *was* incredible so who wouldn't fancy her? She made me see things for what they were and seemed to have an eye for pointing out faults in people, things I hadn't noticed before."

"But Nick, everyone has faults, if we were all perfect the world would be a very boring place. Did she ever mention her own faults, or did she deem herself perfect?"

I sunk. "She said her past had made her 'flawed' - that she 'was spoiled'"

"Spoiled in what way?"

I needed a cigarette. I didn't actually smoke but when I got stressed I would often join Sophie for one. Instead, I picked at the skin around my fingernails.

"It's one of the main things that I fell for," I started, "and I thought I could help her and make her see that her life didn't have to be all about the past; that there *was* a future, a brilliant future, a future for us ... if she could just look forward and not dwell on things."

"But could she realistically do that?"

"Sometimes it seemed like she could, and did. She would be all energised about ideas that I had and go off and research things, only for something else to crop up and get in the way." I was on my feet. I started pacing and my words became less clear. "She couldn't trust men; me; any of us. That my suggestions were all nice ideas but I didn't mean them and ... "

"Sit down. Nick. Please. I think we've talked enough today okay. Come, eat your baguette and then we can pack up and get going."

This day had become a counselling session that would not end even though Carrie was trying to wrap it up. It was now her who didn't want this - didn't want to hear what I was going to say. But I had to tell her what had happened to Sophie, before my head exploded with the weight; something I had kept inside since the very first time we were alone together.

"I need to tell you," I blurted out, "for her to make sense, I really need to tell you."

"Please, Nick let's just leave it until tomorrow, I'm not feeling great and would rather go home – I think I've over done it a bit today, what with venturing out late last night too. Let's just go home huh? Please?" Carrie had tears in her eyes.

Had I been shouting? Going on like a wild thing? Looking like I was having a breakdown right there and then? Isn't this what Carrie wanted? For me to open up and tell her about Sophie. About the reasons why she did the things she did and behaved the way she behaved. Wasn't that what Carrie was trying to get at the very heart of? Or was that me? Had I used this chance, the very slightly open window of opportunity to pour out my emotions? Had I simply cracked?

My heart was beating heavily - so loud it pounded that I couldn't hear myself think. I could hear Sophie's screams between each pump of blood and I desperately wanted them to stop – wanted everything to fall silent so I could think once more. When the screams finally eased, the whispers spoke: "You're responsible," they said.

Carrie was hurriedly packing up the picnic items and then she threw on her clothes over her wet bikini. I feared I would not see her in that bikini ever again. Feared more though, that I might not see her ever again.

"I'm sorry, Carrie," I said, "I guess because it's the first time I have spoken about this, that I want it all out in the open. I'm worried that if I don't do it now I never will." I was already going off the idea of telling her and was thankful that she hadn't allowed me to.

"A little at a time ok?" She was calmer too and came forward and kissed me ever so slightly on the cheek.

I didn't deserve that and yet she had done it to quell the situation and bring us back to the present from my past. I couldn't quite believe her generosity and her empathy. My heart squeezed up into my throat and I cowered away from her. But it was the single most touching moment I had ever experienced. I turned back and held my stare into her eyes for as long as I could, before shying away once more. She was always much better at that game than me. By now I was sure she knew me far greater than I knew her.

There were again rumbles in the distance to thankfully break up the uncomfortable silence as we ambled back through the woods. I wanted to say something more to Carrie - to thank her for being so very sweet and understanding; for reeling me in when I went too far and for giving me security when I needed it most. But I couldn't look her in the eye for I feared I would blush and she would know. The kiss still stung on my cheek - as hard as the slap Sophie had given me just before I dropped her mobile into the boiling water. Her hand still bore pus-filled blisters the day she had committed suicide and I was once again reminded of that moment. However, it wasn't just that. Carrie had left her mark, just as Sophie had done, and the lingering sensation on my cheek again brought back all of the other emotions I had felt when I had first met Sophie. Carrie now knew about our first meeting but that was all I had told her. To go further I would have to go to deeper and darker places in my mind and for that, I would have to be ready and I would have to be calm - the haste at which Carrie wished to leave the pool was evident of that. Tomorrow I would try again with the story of mine and Sophie's first date but I would not force it, nor get angry or sad. I would merely tell it as if I were reading from a book - cold and without emotion. I didn't want Carrie to know that I still missed and loved Sophie, especially now that tonight, in my own bed, I would miss and love Carrie too.

CHAPTER SIX

The Lair

I was woken when the front door slammed. Shortly after, a vehicle started and I went to look out of my bedroom window only see my parents' car drive slowly out of the courtyard. It was the first time I had seen them since the day we arrived. I tried to open the window to shout down to them but the catch was jammed and they were soon out of sight. It was bright daylight. I had slept long and heavy once again.

In the shower I resisted the urge to think too much about Carrie but I was aroused all the same. I had dreamt of her in the night - intimate moments that blurred reality. I felt the need to touch my cheek numerous times as I got changed, before heading downstairs for breakfast.

I poured a huge bowl of cereal and then looking in the fridge, realised we were out of milk. I quickly tuned this into a positive and decided that this would be my first task of the day - to show my parents that I wasn't being all mournful and pathetic and I was at least able to find a nearby shop and purchase some milk. I would also get some snacks for today's venture into the woods to show Carrie that I was making an effort and to apologise for yesterday's outburst. I was looking forward to a day when I wouldn't have to make at least one apology.

I got my rucksack together and then remembered that the cottage we were to visit today was by the sea. This was too great an opportunity to miss and so I trotted out to the garage to find my fishing rod. Before Sophie and I got together, I used to do a lot of fishing. Spurred on by the fact that it gave me a chance to do something outdoors whilst being on my own - fishing and myself were always going to form a strong bond. Whilst my mates were off playing football or cricket, I would simply jump on the train or bus and head to the coast and find a solitary place to fish. I would spend all day there with my own thoughts and it was in those times that I begun to string stories together - ones that I would eventually write. I managed to get a short story published via an *iTunes App* and was asked to read it in the school assembly -something which I declined. It was the first time both of my parents had sat me down to say how proud they were of me and that they had shown all of their friends, although I doubt that either of them had actually read it. The writing, along with the fishing, eased up once I met Sophie. Her demand on my time too great for isolated days on my own. With Carrie however, I had the feeling that she would be excitable about my attempts at trying to catch us lunch.

As I eagerly approached the garage my heart sunk. I remembered that the other day it had been locked and the key was no-where to be found. I hopefully tried the handle anyway but just as I knew, it wouldn't budge. I hunched my way back inside, tripping over something in the porch. As I turned around to kick it, I stopped myself. My eyes opened wide - I couldn't believe my luck. Grabbing the cloth-covered long thin item I quickly pulled at the tied strings. I knew what was in there but I just had to see it. Low and behold there it was, my two piece fishing rod, a spinning rod in fact that I had used extensively three summers before. Not only that, but behind it my fishing reel and tackle box filled with new, unopened, lures, hooks and weights. I recalled that only a week before meeting Sophie, I had bought a load of new fishing gear with the money the publication had given me for that short story. I whispered to anyone who might be listening, "Thank you."

A knock at the door startled me, bringing me out of my nostalgia. It was Carrie. She looked red in the face.

"Hi, Nick," she said, shifting uneasily.

"Hi, you alright?" I noticed that she wouldn't look me in the eye.

"I want to say this now ok, I'm sorry I kissed you on the cheek yesterday. Please can we forget I did that?"

"Sure ... " I started before looking at the fishing rod. "We can forget about it, but I don't wish to. It was the most ... " *Not so brave now are we?* " ... it was the best thing you could have done." Okay not totally romantic but at least I told her how I felt. Kind of.

Carrie said nothing, so I started again, this time trying to explain myself fully, "It snapped me out of ... well let's just say, Carrie I really appreciated it." I found myself using her name more and more, just as she did with mine. Was it an affectionate thing? I didn't know? I then did something rather bizarre. I ruffled her hair as if she were a cheeky child who had played a prank on me. I felt a need to touch her and make her feel secure. But I didn't want skin on skin for that would surely give the game away.

Carrie laughed - it had worked, thankfully.

"I'm sorry, Nick, I'd been awake in the night worried about what you thought of me. I don't normally do that sort of thing. It just felt right."

I then realised that what she had done was actually even more than I originally assumed. She kissed me on the cheek to calm me yes, but she had also done it because she had wanted to. *Wanted to kiss me.* Maybe it was the sadness she saw and the love I was able to project that did it or maybe it was just a feeling she always had - I didn't really care. This girl had kissed me because she wanted to and that was far better in my book than kissing me because she thought I needed it.

"Well it worked and I'm very grateful," I said, rather smug. I grabbed my rucksack and fishing stuff and ushered her out of the porch. If I was inside and alone with her I wouldn't be able to resist the urges rising within me.

"Can we go to a shop on the way please?" I spoke far too loud and with too much energy.

"Nick, the woods are that way and the shop is that way." Her arms outstretched perpendicular. "Besides, what do you need?"

"I need some milk and some snacks for us today."

"That's very thoughtful of you, but I've got it covered. Sandwiches, sausage rolls and pork pies okay? Not the healthiest but so what huh?"

"Ah fantastic, I love them all." Could she be any more perfect, any more of the time? This had gone beyond developing a crush stage. She was the girl I had wanted Sophie to be; everything and more.

"But if it's not enough, then I'll catch you something with that ropey old rod of yours." Again, I felt my heart in my throat. Carrie was continuing to say the right things.

"I feel a competition coming on." I bucked, itching to get to the cottage. Again I clumsily climbed the roots down to the wooded path, whilst Carrie jumped.

"Did you hear the storm last night again?" she asked.

"Only what we heard coming back yesterday," I replied, licking my salty top lip.

"It was a whopper, and going to get even worse over the next day or so apparently."

"Did you investigate?"

"No, not last night, I was too busy watching an old vampire movie."

"Really? They're my favourite, which one?" I was curious as to what she perceived as being 'old' in movie terms.

"Brides of Dracula," she said nonchalantly.

I remembered it as quite a risqué piece from Hammer Films, featuring everything you want in a vampire movie, albeit it without Dracula himself. I was instantly impressed - first for watching such a classic and second for remembering the title of it. Sophie wouldn't have done either. And then in my arousal, recalling a movie we had once watched together, I remembered something she used to do and what I had always found the most alluring of acts. She had done this for the first time when we were watching Black Swan whilst in a vamp-like state.

"What's your ultimate fantasy?" Sophie asked, snuggling up to me as the movie played. Before she allowed me a chance to reply, she urgently carried on.

"I bet it's to have two girls isn't it? To have them both fuck you and each other."

She was never one to mince her words, but this was only our third date. Speechless I watched her stand over me, pull aside her tiny lace knickers with one hand and begin masturbating with the other. Right on cue the lesbian scene appeared in the movie. I caught glimpses of it between her legs and then over her shoulder as she turned away from me to watch for herself. She pulled me out of my boxer-shorts and slid down onto me, all the while fixated on the film in our virtual foursome. Just before Sophie orgasmed she said that if I wanted to, she would do that for me, for only recently, a female friend of hers had licked her out. I came harder than I had ever done before. Three hours later, we were still fucking.

.   .   .

I've masturbated about that night many times over, and now I had an erection so hard I simply couldn't hide it. I was disgusted for allowing that memory to turn me on once more. I took off my rucksack and carried it in front of me. This was one day I was determined not to allow Sophie to spoil. I would not continue with the story from yesterday, I would start afresh, blank her from my mind and dispel the voices. But just as the pool had done - on arrival at the cottage the voices grew louder and she would again rush to the forefront of my mind.

.   .   .

It looked just like the cottage Sophie and I had dreamt about getting. A place where we could shut out the world and begin to grow our own little family - somewhere isolated where no one else could hurt us.

Although this particular cottage was just a derelict shell, I could tell it meant so much more to Carrie and I could sense a feeling of magic and calm as we approached the unhinged, waist-high gate, resting against the small, crooked remains of a fence; the words, 'Wolf's Lair' remained faintly etched within the wood.

"Cute huh?" said Carrie. "I've always dreamed of one day owning this place and doing it up to make it my very own ... although it's just a brick building and empty inside I still imagine what it once was ... and might again be."

Carrie was speaking poetically once more. I found that when she did this, the world seemed dreamy, childlike and altogether more innocent. Nostalgia washed over me and I fought back the tears.

"Is there really nothing inside?" I asked.

"There's a table and chairs. My dad and I would sit in there sometimes and keep out of the rain."

I gave her a puzzled look.

"He would bring me fishing here. Mum was never interested."

"Come, I'll show you the fishing spot in a bit but first let's go inside."

Carrie fiddled with the lock. "We replaced this last summer, dad and I, the hinges too, but the door's still a bit of a bugger. I refuse to change it."

The door creaked under the heavy, rotten, deadwood strain but opened fully. I shivered as sunlight crept into the room. In the hazy blur I could make out a simple wooden table and two matching chairs. I exhaled on entering the cottage as things became clearer. The table and chairs had been recently painted: white and glossy. There was a small pot plant in the centre, vibrant and moist, housing a simple golden flower, which faced the only window opposite me. Carrie grabbed a cloth out of her rucksack and soaked it in a bucket of water just inside the doorway, before heading back outside. She then appeared at the window, rubbing delicately at the simple, single pane of glass. More light entered the room and I could see the cottage in all its glory. The bare stonework - heavily-weathered - housing spider webs and moss-thickened at one end to form an oversized fireplace. There were ashes and blackened wood inside. A wire-mesh with a handle was propped up next to it. Something was stuck to the grill.

It was a perfect little getaway. I could imagine me and Sophie running away to spend time in this place – our own little hideout where no-one could find us.

The quiet of the cottage was only interrupted by the feint hum of insects and a not so distant fold of wavelets.

I sat down at the table for no reason at all. Carrie came back inside the cottage to join me.

"Cool huh?" she finally said, breaking the silence.

"Uh-huh."

"Marshmallows!" she shouted, jerking me from my heavy thoughts. "We should bring marshmallows next time."

"And hot chocolate." I said quietly, under my breath.

"Yes, yes! Late at night, when it gets dark. It'll be very exciting!"

I was enamoured by her charms once more. Again, she had helped rid my morbid self-torture. Her energy and her need for adventure kept me on my toes. My reluctance to follow her was waning. I had begun to find 'me' once more and the bursts of self-pity were becoming short and brief, yet the intensity still held firm.

She pulled out a couple of half squashed sandwiches wrapped in cling film.

"Sorry, was in a bit of rush this morning and there wasn't much in the fridge."

I examined my buttered sandwich: Tomato ketchup. It was my childhood favourite.

"These look ace." I managed, with a grin.

Carrie giggled and wolfed down hers before she bolted out of the chair, smacked her lips against mine and hastily went out of the door, grabbing the fishing rod on the way.

"I almost forgot! Come Nick, we'll miss the tide."

Getting up I placed my sandwich on the table, wiped red sauce from my mouth and quickly followed. The child in me was there for all to see. Carrie beamed an accomplished smile, grabbed my hand and yanked me out the gate. The noise of water being sucked over stones increased as we entered the trees to our left and as we ventured over a cacophony of rocks, I could finally see the sea. The intense smell of salty air engulfed me - warming me further. The tide was rapidly forced through the gully and into the small crevasses beneath our feet. Carrie scurried around the gully and further to a headland overlooking deeper water. Even though she still had the rod in her hand I was lagging behind. We both fought with grip on wet rocks and eventually I joined her at the headland just as she dextrously finished assembling a string of feathers onto the line.

"Don't laugh if I fuck this up, it's been a while." She was grinning whilst planting her feet as best she could, widening her stance in the process and as she pulled back with her cast, her tongue protruded over her lips.

My stomach fluttered. All of a sudden I was finally doing something I did before meeting Sophie. Something I loved doing and had given up on doing to spend more time with her. Sophie didn't trust me enough to go and do things on my own and the one time I persuaded her to come along with me, she had hated it - complaining of the cold despite the disposable barbecue I'd brought with us and flask of tea I had made. Again, things I did to try were never enough. I was never enough.

Carrie was so very different, she didn't even screw up the first cast, which I was sure she would.

"Not bad for a girl huh?" she beamed.

She began reeling in, changing the speed of retrieval. Looking over at me every few seconds.

I swallowed hard. "You're okay I guess."

Smiling, she sped up the rate until the lures were out of the water.

"Now your turn."

I avidly took the rod from her and got myself into position. Just as I was about to cast out, I closed my eyes for a second and launched the line as far as I could.

"Not bad ... for a boy," she smirked.

I puff out my cheeks, unaware as to how long I'd been holding my breath for. The feathers hadn't quite gone in the direction I wanted them too, but it was good enough – all things considered.

We continued to take it in turns to cast out and reel in and with the pressure off we were getting further and more accurate each time. Carrie made a couple of quips although she never actually said anything, until finally:

"Fish on."

"Yeah right."

"Fish on, Nick," she insisted.

I couldn't believe how calm she was. At first anyhow. Her little feet soon began dancing as the rod fluttered under strain.

"Fish on!" I shouted. "Ha-ha, brilliant!"

She bent over, giggling away whilst still trying to reel it in.

"Keep the rod high!" But she was already doing everything I would have done - only in a far more alluring way. As much as the fish itself was hooked, I was also beginning to find myself in her grasp; she was as Sophie had been – intoxicating.

I grabbed the mackerel as it left the water. Its green back was almost fluorescent against the dark stripes and its underbelly: a shimmering silver in the low sun. As I studied it, the intensity and the strength of which it fought to get out of my grasp was altogether too familiar. I wanted desperately to bash its head over the nearest rock - to stop its struggle, its torture, its foreboding, but instead I looked at Carrie. She smiled and nodded. I crouched down and gently threw the fish back into the sea. I stood up, feeling lightheaded whilst looking around me. The stillness and the quiet only broken when Carrie approached. We kissed long, deep and hard. I felt my heart weep as my soul filled my veins. No longer feeling alone - I felt solace.

"Ew!" she said, grabbing my hand. "Fish gunk!" She swapped her grip to my other hand, but the remnants remained.

"What now?" I forced myself to stay in the present.

"We have time to bypass the graveyard if you wish?"

I was gobsmacked. The whole time I'd wanted to go and Carrie had simply dismissed it out of hand, yet now when I assumed it was never going to happen she actually brought it up.

I spoke quietly, "We really don't have to."

95

"No it's ok, I think with us both there it would be fine - comforting even?"

Her tone was far too inquisitive.

"What's the catch?"

"Catch?"

"I'm just surprised you suggested it."

"Well I'm open to new things."

My thoughts propelled straight back to the past: Sophie's constant attempts at sexually shocking me - turning me on and into a horny wreck. When she had me like that I just said yes to whatever she asked of me, as there was always a bargaining tool coming from her end: a run to the shop for fags; me to do her homework; a new dress; tickets for her and a friend (whom I'd never met) to a festival etc.

Well I'm open to new things.

I was blushing, but once again craving. I had been so goddamn asexual since Sophie split up from me but now my stomach was doing somersaults thinking things best not thought of.

Carrie cut the atmosphere: "Maybe it's time you finished telling me what you started at the pool."

It wasn't even a question. And then I got it - we could only get it on if she knew what truly happened to Sophie. And so I had to tell her - what had really happened and not what she might have read online. I couldn't avoid it any longer; I guessed I owed her it.

CHAPTER SEVEN
The Suicide

As the cemetery came into view I noticed Carrie stiffen, her pace ever slower, as if walking with the chains of Jacob Marley. She sat in the same place in which she jumped me. For what seemed like months ago - was in fact only two days. Her position was such that she kept her back to the graves as much as possible, yet was still able to look over her right shoulder, towards them. I sat opposite her, facing the broken headstones. As much as I would have rather gone in to investigate, I pushed on with the task in hand.

"How much do you want to know?" The hypothetical tone in my voice, and her own continued silence, spoke volumes. So I pushed on, "I was aware that Sophie had frequently been playing around. What I wasn't sure was with whom and how many? I just knew it was more than one;

possibly several. Ever since the incident when she had burnt herself with the boiling water my suspicions were no longer unfounded. The initialised name she had received in that text proved things that deep down, I already knew. Following this I gained access, don't ask me how, to her personal messages on *Facebook* and her *iCloud* photos. It was obvious I was dating someone who I really could not fulfil physically or emotionally. I had challenged her on many issues, told her that she needed to see a counsellor and that I felt she was unstable. She reacted exactly as I thought she would."

"What exactly are you trying to say?" Sophie asked.

"You're unsettling me Soph, I can't be with you. I don't trust you."

"What? All because of you snooping at my texts? You're fucking out of order, you know that."

*"I think you have a problem." I started slowly and calmly, "You use people, you flaunt yourself physically and emotionally onto people and make them putty in your hands." I flicked the loose fitting, low cut top she was wearing. If she was at the right angle, her nipples were viewable through the thin, delicate fabric. She was **often** at the right angle.*

"You're jealous. Men and women find me attractive, there's not much I can do about that!" She crossed her arms.

"That's understandable." I replied, knowing full well that she was right. "But I also know you're acting on it."

Her face twisted. Open mouthed she blushed and looked down to her left. I was studying her, looking for further proof. I desperately wanted to look away and pretend there wasn't any.

"Think what you want, I know you think I'm rough, I can tell by the way you look at me."

For once, it was me that decided to stay silent, not able to meet her burning stare. I mimicked her previous expression, before mumbling, "You could be so much more."

"Fuck you, Nick." she snapped, rising to her feet. "I don't have to listen to this. I'm absolutely fine, stop analysing me."

"Please don't go, I can help you."

"Just who do you think you are?"

And before I could respond she was out the door and running down the street. I made a half-hearted attempt to go after her, but there were too many people about. People that would undoubtedly take her side if we started arguing in the street. I saw her turn left and over the road without looking, and then she was into the park and out of sight. I wondered if I would ever see her again.

Several weeks passed and my parents were out at another one of their conventions. It was always the first weekend of the month when they would simply pack up on a Friday evening and head off - a quick kiss goodbye if I was lucky and then the usual, "See you Sunday night!" but it was always Monday when I would actually see them. I sat up watching nothing on TV that could keep my attention and at the same time was logged into Facebook and Twitter looking for clues about Sophie: what she was up to, her whereabouts - that sort of thing. But nothing. It was 4am when I finally decided to go to bed, yet as I got to the top of the stairs the house phone rang. I knew it was her. She'd lasted longer without me than I thought, but not much. I answered immediately, "It's me", she whimpered. "Please ... please can I see you, I need help."

"Where are you? I'll come get you." I blurted out. It was raining heavily outside and in her state of mind there was no way I'd let her spend more time alone wandering around in the dark than she needed - than I needed.

"I'm already here," she replied; there was an echoed knock at the door. I scurried over and struggled with the lock before throwing the door open to her. She looked wrong, very wrong.

Her hair, now short and red, was dripping blood coloured dye down her neck and into her white, wet, see-through top which clung to her, revealing every contour of her naked flesh underneath. Her jeans were black, or dark blue - I couldn't tell and she was holding a single black stiletto in her left hand. Her feet were bare and her face was tucked into the nape of her neck. Her eyes lit only by the glow of her mobile phone and *the cigarette, shaking in her hand. She was shivering uncontrollably as she attempted time and time again to shut off our phone conversation.*

I pulled her into me, into the warmth of the house and pressed myself against her. Within seconds she was on top of me, tearing at my clothes before desperately trying to put myself inside her - eventually pulling down her trousers just enough to do so. I came as soon as I had fully penetrated her; emptying myself inside her for the first time, and, also for the first time, she herself failed to cum. As I hurriedly began to pull out, she clenched and held me steady for a moment before rolling off me onto her back, cupping her right hand between her legs. She lay still, staring at the ceiling, her eyes fixed; unblinking. A single tear ran down her right cheek.

"I want it to be yours Nick," she said, twisting away from me, onto her side. "You'd be good for it."

Quickly I got to my feet, half-pulling up my trousers in the process. Rushing to the bathroom sink I washed myself repeatedly until I became sore, gagging in the process. My stomach was in knots and I was crying, yet I still wanted her to come to me: to check on me, to see if I was all right, but she never did. Back in the lounge she was sat on the sofa, still holding herself between her legs. Her jeans were on the floor and she still wore the wet, white top that revealed everything. As I approached her she pulled a cushion against her chest and leaned forward to pick up her jeans. Instead of putting them on, she pulled a skimpy pair of white silk

102

knickers from the back pocket and slid herself into them. Her right hand was damp and a part of me remained in her hair as she swept it out of her eyes.

"What do you think then?" she asked.

"About what?"

"Us having a baby."

"I think you need to see someone."

"Yeah but only when I know for sure, I could get one of those tests, I know how they work."

"That's not the sort of person I meant Sophie." I bowed my head but kept eye contact.

"Fuck off, just where do you get off?"

"Look at yourself, look at what just happened."

"I think you'll find I'm just fine thank you very much — stop telling me what to do. I gave you sex, it's what you wanted wasn't it. Maybe even a baby too — you know you want my baby."

She was even worse than I could possibly have imagined. I was scared and I realised that now I desperately needed help.

"What you doing?" she asked as I picked up the landline.

"I just need to phone my dad, I've forgotten ... I've forgotten to tell him about a message he had earlier."

"Since when would that bother you?"

"Please Sophie, I just want to do the right thing."

103

"You've always been wet. Stick up for yourself for a change, you know they don't give a shit."

"And you do?"

"Well I'm here aren't I?"

I slammed the phone down. I was done. Beaten. Sophie was going to get it one way or the other. The truth. About her and what she really was.

"Okay Sophie, enough."

"What do you mean enough? You love ... "

"Stop, just fucking stop." The taut, tightly wound band finally snapped.

She got up off the sofa to leave – her face blotchy.

"No, fuck you Sophie, you're going to listen to this." I grabbed her and threw her back down onto the couch. When she winced, I moved towards her apologetically but then she came at me - fists flying, growling, spitting. I held both her hands and as I pinned them to her sides she threw her head upwards into my face. My top lip instantly felt hot and I could taste sweet syrup. I didn't have the time to consider just what part of me was bleeding as she tried to throw her head into me again but this time I caught hold of her throat and threw her back onto the sofa with so much force it rocked onto its hind legs. Sophie grabbed the cushions around her, covering as much of herself as she could. Eventually I relaxed my hands,

standing over her I had somehow resisted her invitation; instead I would hurt her much worse.

Calmly I said, "There's something very wrong with you. Something evil."

She peered at me through the cushions. Even though the gap was small I could see her frowning. Her hatred bore into me and I was genuinely scared as to what might happen if I carried on with her assessment. I pressed two of my fingers to my front teeth - both were still in place. It had only been ten minutes since she had arrived dripping wet at my door and I had welcomed her in. Things could sadly never get back to the way they once were. Not now.

"I know people," I started. "People that can help you, therapists, counsellors, that type of thing."

"I went already." This wasn't the answer I was expecting. "When we first broke up and you said my behaviour was **erratic**. You told me to see someone then!"

"How come you never told me?" I asked.

"We weren't together. The lad, the one I dumped you for, I was with him then."

She wasn't lying to protect herself anymore, she was being honest, finally honest, but again not for my sake, but for hers. She knew she could hurt me with it.

"I'm just confirming what you already knew Nick, don't look at me like that, I don't need your pity." But I wasn't pitying her, of that I was sure.

"So was it me or him that made you see a therapist?"

"It was a counsellor actually and what does it matter anyway, she said I was fine and that I should box up all my bad memories and float them down the river and make a fresh start because I deserved better."

She had conned her counsellor too.

"You obviously weren't honest with her then."

"I told her what needed to be told. The meeting was about me and basically I welcome in too many bad influences. She said I have a mothering instinct and want to look after people and give them what they want, regardless of how I feel."

Conned her good and proper.

"It's funny hey? Good old little me and my mothering instincts. Turns out her mother died when she was young. I helped her blank out the memory for a bit but now she's another one that won't leave me the fuck alone. Maybe I should do that as a job. Fancy giving me the money to study for it? Ha-ha I'll pay you back one day, perleease!"

I wasn't just scared anymore I was freaked out. This mothering instinct she was talking about resulted in her having a termination a short while before meeting me. A story she had never wanted to elaborate on.

106

And as for the counsellor, just what the fuck was with everyone? My groin ached as I glared at her. I had never been more disgusted.

"Did you tell her about the abortion you had?" I scowled.

"What do you mean, Nick, I was a virgin before we met," she laughed.

"I think I deserve the truth Sophie. How much of it all is bullshit?"

She snapped. Launching herself off the sofa, but not towards me, nor the door, but the kitchen. I ran in after her, shaking and crying. As she got to the sink and pulled open the cutlery drawer I skidded to a halt on the beige kitchen tiles, just a few feet away from her. As she pulled out the biggest blade in there I backed away.

"You think I'm a liar huh? That all this is bullshit? Just who have you told? Well fuck you, Nick, fuck you and deal with this."

The first carve into her left wrist made no sound whatsoever, but when she attacked it a second time, there were snaps and piercing screams as her whole hand went limp and she splattered the sink as she bent over it. She then tried to place the knife into her wounded hand but it dropped to the floor. As the blood began to pour I stayed motionless; my bladder emptied and I could taste acid. Sophie had the knife between her knees and was forcing her good arm against it. Finally I ran over and picked her up. The knife was in her hand once again, hacking away at her near dismembered left hand.

"Finish the job!" she spat at me. "Try and explain this to your fucking conscience."

As we both slumped to the floor she whispered one final thing: "I win. I always do." And then everything went black.

A short while later, I don't know how long, I stirred to find her still in my arms with the warm blood continuing to flow. It was then that I ran out of the house, yelling as I crossed the pavement before collapsing to my knees in the middle of the quiet street. I looked around me, desperate for anyone to come running. I could see innocent children playing in the park just a few yards away, completely unaware of what was happening. I screamed louder and then finally they came; not towards me, but towards the blood-drenched figure crawling out of the front door of my house, her arm with the flaccid wrist outstretched towards me before finally she collapsed and went still; only then, was I noticed by the crowd.

CHAPTER EIGHT
The Graveyard Part I

"Fucking Hell, Nick."

"I know."

"Christ it's no wonder you're messed up."

"Cheers," I replied.

"Sorry, you know I don't mean it like that."

"I know, but I am, it's simple really. I can't fucking believe it. Why didn't I help? I was just so scared. I panicked. I froze. The time she needed me the most I failed her."

"There's a cry for help *and* then there's something altogether more determined, more final, I'm afraid, Nick."

"But she would be in the hospital now, with proper doctors - not some influential, just out of college counsellor."

"People have to be responsible for their own decisions, she made choices and couldn't deal with them. You shouldn't have to pick up the pieces and try to rectify the error of their ways."

"She obviously needed help though."

"Obviously. You were the closest person emotionally attached to her. I believe that to be so. Therefore it was never going to be possible for you to be *that* person."

"I don't get it?"

"The ones we are closest to, are sometimes the ones we hurt the most. The relationship was destroyed when you tried to fix her."

"So it is all of my fault?"

"No. It's all of her fault. You weren't the one who brought all of the baggage into the relationship and threw it on her doorstep."

Doorstep. My doorstep. Sophie. Pointing. Dying.

"So what happened then?" Carrie quizzed.

"Huh?"

"After she came out of your house?"

"I blacked out again. Those people in the street set upon me and then ... nothing."

"They attacked you? It sounds like you need to speak with the police. Yet you're here in one piece, not battered nor bruised. So considering the trauma you went through it sounds like you fainted or just, I don't know, collapsed? You know, in total shock of what had happened. It's much harder for people to attack someone when they're already on the floor and defenceless."

"I don't know, again, I don't fucking know? I'm just worried that with my family dragging me here, not that I gave any resistance, makes me a suspect? No? If people at the scene were ready to judge me, then what chance do I have with those that came after?"

"It sounds like you did the right thing, or you got lucky. Either way if Sophie's lynch mob were out for blood, your blood, then coming here was the best thing your family could've done for you."

"Yes I understand that, but these were just your average folk off the street and it was outside *my* house, not hers."

"People get scared and people are sheep. They react when they see something. Something they don't understand. And of course, they're always more inclined to help the girl."

"A parenting instinct." I whispered.

"What was that?"

"It's just something I've been thinking about lately. Sophie was extremely up and down, always giving off this persona of vulnerability. It's why I ... "

"She sounded bipolar." Carrie interrupted.

"That's exactly what I thought!" I shouted. "Although it took a fair bit of research to get me there."

"Well then again it backs up that it's not your fault at all. It's a chemical thing, I've read all about it."

"But there are things which can trigger this off. Maybe my meddling and my insistence on her to seek help only served to heighten her discomfort and agitated her to the extreme, causing her to end it."

"Maybe she was so fucked in the head, Nick that she was always going to do this. It was her fate."

"There's just so much more I wish I knew."

"Sometimes not knowing is better."

"It's the not knowing that's driving me crazy. I think by the way she reacted, some things, well they just must have been true."

"Or maybe she reacted like that because none of it was?"

"How do you mean?"

"I guess no-one ever truly knows someone."

112

"But why does that have to be? Why do people need to have secrets from one another? If people have unequivocal love for each other they would accept them ... warts and all," I opened my palms to Carrie, almost as Sophie had done to me, "That's what I *had* with her."

"Which is maybe why she had such a hold over you? People shouldn't be able to do exactly as they please ... knowingly hurting others in the process, thriving on that pain and all the while getting deeper inside that person's head, tightening their grip."

"I just loved her." I said.

"I know. And as much as love is supposed to be the ultimate emotion, it's not always a positive thing. It deceives us into making irrational decisions and choices. We end up with the wrong people because of it and it eats away at us from within."

"So what's better? Just sticking to something that's safe and therefore never falling in love?"

"No ... I guess not," she dwelled. "I think that would be even worse." Carrie lifted herself up to be seated on the dry stonewall. Her feet now dangling as she clicked her heels and looked over her shoulder towards the gravestones. I pulled myself up alongside her but instead faced the cemetery.

113

"You must have looked her up on the internet ... since she ... " her voice tailed off.

"Whenever I typed her name in, it just mentioned the suicide." I replied. Carrie shot me a puzzled look. "I couldn't get past the headlines:

'Teen Dies In Suspected Suicide'.

'Girl Attempts To Cut Off Her Own Hands'.

'Blood Bath In Broad Daylight'.

I guess it's why we left so abruptly."

"When did you last look on the *WEB*?"

"The day we travelled here. I sneaked a look on my mum's phone on the boat just before we lost signal. I was actually grateful as the longer I had it the more I wanted to read into the articles, other than just the headlines that *Google* was showing up."

"Why didn't you want to find out more?"

"I didn't ... I couldn't handle reading about her death. The intimate details surrounding it. The fact some of me was still inside her as she lay dead at the side of the street." I shuddered. "The headlines were enough. The girl I loved killed herself and *I'm* to blame."

"You're *not*, Nick. You weren't the one holding the knife, and you weren't the one cutting into her flesh. There were so many things wrong with her - I can tell that from the things you've told me. Yet I'm sure there's still more that you're bottling up and there's probably even more you'll never *ever* know about."

"I've resigned myself to that fact."

"And that's what really pains you isn't it?" Carrie took my hand in hers and put her chin onto my shoulder. "You did dwell on this earlier."

"It's just the not knowing." I reiterated.

"I understand. But some things are better kept in the dark; some things you're better off not knowing." Again reiteration.

I shivered and was welling up, "I guess you can't change the past."

"Are you going to be alright to go home tonight? I'm worried about leaving you on your own."

"I'm exhausted." I admitted.

"It's the first time you've spoken about it isn't it?"

I nodded.

"What is it with you and your parents? I don't get how they can be so uncaring?"

"I just think it's more about them not being bothered. You know, I'm too much hassle, that sort of thing. If it doesn't fit into their scheme of things, well then, it's something they can't be arsed with."

"Have they really not spoken to you about it? They must have met her?"

"I already said. *No*! But yes they did meet her but only fleetingly. Just the times when she'd come to mine though, slightly earlier than we'd arranged, before my parents had gone away for the weekend. My mum was somewhat cautious of her, but they never said more than two words to one another. It wasn't unusual. My parents had never said more than two words to any of my friends."

"So how do you know she was cautious of her?"

"I think it was because she only saw her just as they were leaving. I took it as a bit of a dig at me as well. 'You could've waited until we'd actually left before you get your friends around for a party' she had said, in front of both of us. 'It's only one friend' I had corrected her. 'I'm his girlfriend!' Sophie had said, which made me smile, before my mother looked her up and down, turned back towards me and shaking her head. The next couple of weekends they went away, the same routine ensued. It was like Sophie was sticking two fingers up at them and I loved her for doing so."

"Which made your bond stronger."

"Yeah. It did."

"So your parents are no use to us then?"

"No."

"They'll come looking you know."

I shook my head. "If they wanted to speak to me they would've done already. I just think they want to pretend that the whole thing never happened. Which suits me I guess as I'd rather leave them out of it."

"No, not your parents. The police."

I shrugged.

"I'm amazed you got to Jersey without them tracking you down beforehand."

"I know that too."

"Maybe your parents' influences have paid off." Carrie nodded, "For now."

"Care to share details?" I asked.

"I saw you arrive. *Jack and Kate Guest as our new neighbours.* Who'd have thought?"

"Stop smiling."

"And their cute son came with them," she blushed.

117

I joined her.

"I guess we'll just have to figure it out if they come."

"Agreed."

"Right now though, it's the two of us against the world yeah?"

"I'm happy with that."

"Good. That makes me happy too. Come, let's explore this place of yours." Carrie hastily turned towards the graveyard, stopping to look at her feet before tiptoeing through the gap in the wall.

"I thought it was ours?"

"No, the rest of it is ours, you can have this place to yourself. I'm not especially partial to graveyards thanks."

"Well we don't have to ..." I went to follow her regardless but also stopped at the entrance. The putrid smell coming from within was disturbing to say the least and I was trying not to gag.

"Not so sure now, are you?"

"Hmm, no. It skinks."

"That'll be the rotting flesh of the undead.

"Thanks for that."

"We're here now, so let's do this. Besides, who knows how long we've got before they come?"

"The zombies?" I laughed.

"Better them than the poli ... " Carrie's smile quickly disappeared and eventually she gasped, "They ... the zombies." She looked at me ashen faced, "They're already here."

CHAPTER NINE

The Graveyard Part II

"What? What is it?" I hurried through the gateway, holding my breath, yet still I wanted to wretch. As I got closer to her, my legs grew heavy. So heavy, that before I had made it to within ten yards of Carrie I was on my knees. My eyes sunk to the back of my skull and everything went grey. I was conscious just long enough for Carrie's warning.

"Keep away, Nick; keep away!"

When I woke up, Carrie was nowhere to be seen. I coughed acid as I sat up against one of the gravestones, midway into the cemetery. Behind me was where she had warned me about going. I edged myself out and peered around the corner of the tomb. Carrie was knelt beside the newest of the graves. Her hand was on her throat, her skin deathly pale but now with sodden cheeks.

"I thought this place   was obsolete?" I called.

"Oh, Nick ... so did I." She turned to look at me and instantly I knew.

END OF PART ONE

PART TWO

PROLOGUE

For a long while I remained sitting, staring at Carrie, who in turn was staring at the grave. Even from this distance I could tell she was shaking. I waited a while, thinking hard, trying to piece together the last few hours, days, weeks even? But I couldn't fathom the timescale from when we, or rather my parents, actually arrived in Jersey – let alone when my death occurred. All I could contemplate was that ever since I had been here, it had felt like a dream. Time had seemed to have stood still in parts, yet at other moments, disappeared altogether, and right now, I couldn't recall what happened from the moment I ran out into the street - only to turn around and see Sophie crawl out of my house behind me in a blood-bath. I concentrated hard: sirens, people on me. Then the next thing, I was in the car on the way to the port with my mother talking about the local press and picking glances at me in the back.

"I don't remember dying." I blurted out, not to anyone in particular. Of course, Carrie was the only person in vocal range and thinking about it, the only person I could recall having interaction with for the last ... however many days.

There was a murmur. Carrie was whispering. She was holding herself - her arms hugging her twitching body.

Again, I didn't know what to do. Here I was, obviously alive and breathing and feeling everything emotionally and physically, sitting against one gravestone and yet, twenty yards away from me, Carrie was bent double on the floor staring at my own crypt.

Zombie.

I looked at Carrie and questioned if I was hungry. No, I wasn't. In fact I couldn't remember eating or drinking anything since I had arrived in Jersey. I had felt thirsty, extremely thirsty and drunk gallons of water to get rid of the dryness in my mouth, but nothing had stayed down. The dryness had eventually passed and with it, the desire to put anything to my lips - other than Carrie.

Tomato Sauce sandwiches, didn't I have these?

I stopped the thought dead.

124

Dead.

"How?" A murmur twenty yards away. "Fresh, filled-fresh, new." Carrie screamed and looked at me for the first time since the revelation. "How?!"

I snapped out of my delusions of appetite and realised that the only desires I had for Carrie were pure affection. Sexual.

"I don't ... " I start, "I don't ... " I can offer no more.

"Think, Nick for fuck's sake, think."

"Surely I would have ..."

"Don't you dare, Nick, don't you ... "

"What? You think I know what the fuck is going on?"

Silence. Something I couldn't stand, as this was what the voices came. But this time my head was full of questions - my own questions and it was only my own voice, over and over again:

I'm dead?

I'm dead?

I'm dead.

"It says here you were a beloved child." Carrie's voice: calm, soft.

The silence ... broken.

"What ... what else does it say?" I beg, "Carrie please." Anything but the quiet returning, even the reading of my own epitaph whilst me, the zombie, listened.

"Our Beloved Child, Taken Too Early From Us."

A lump in my throat.

How original.

Carrie went on, "May Your Dreams Give You In Death, What They Couldn't Do In Life."

I wanted the reading to stop.

"Rest In Peace, Nick."

CHAPTER ONE

The Awakening

For the whole of my short life I had never managed to figure out who I should've been. Pulled in so many directions by people the closest to me as a tool to get what *they* wanted out of life - I never really found my *own* place.

My mother and father had used me as a trophy, and my only girlfriend, as a fall back option of dependability. It was only really my friends that had never wanted anything from me other than just 'me'. But those friendships soon vanished once Sophie had come onto the scene and was yet another thing I would never be sure of - each blaming one another - again a closure I knew would never be granted. No-one had come as close to me as Sophie had. I let her into my mind wholeheartedly and this is why I felt so pathetic and so discouraged to form any normal relationship since meeting her for the first time. My trust had been broken. The unguarded barriers I had with her as we experimented together so innocently now seemed like filthy, disgusting memories. I was ashamed I had given myself so totally to her. My body, mind and soul. Yet each time I remembered those periods of debauchery, the initial memory sent my pulse racing and heart pounding, before I was quickly snapped back into the stark clarity of her insipid ways which turned the lustful nostalgia into a remorse so lewd, it made me sick to my stomach. As I looked at Carrie through the tufts of tall grass that lay between the tombstones, I remembered just how my friends had been before Sophie's influence had driven me away from them - and them from me. But deep down, this had been my choice, my decision. Carrie had been a true friend to me since I arrived in Jersey and I had to acknowledge that. I needed her to know how much I appreciated her whimsical ways, how much she has picked me up from the depths of despair I had found myself in, and finally, how much I was falling in love with her. For all of her independence and differing views to Sophie, she still reminded me of her: the sexual energy, the ability to melt my heart with the things she spoke about and the twinkle in her eye when there was an edginess to our intimate conversations. I was scared of her for all the wrong reasons and you could say I desired her for the very same. But she wasn't Sophie, and in equal quantities that had to be a good thing; a hopeful thing; a lasting thing. But then I remembered:

Zombie.

The contradicting thoughts in my mind had blurred what was now the very urgent topic that I was dead. Dead yet still here, talking to people – well, talking to Carrie, and continuing to live my life as if death had never taken me.

I thought long and hard, trying to figure out exactly the time when I had become disconnected physically from this world and yet I couldn't. I thought about eating, drinking, sleeping and breathing. For each of them I had no answer. I recalled being so utterly ravenous, yet not being able to keep anything down. It dawned on me that I hadn't eaten or drank since I arrived in Jersey. The last thing I actually recall was an hour before Sophie had arrived that night, the last night. A simple piece of hot buttered toast. *The only food that day.* In the weeks after we split I lived on toast and cereal. That was all I could recall.

Sleeping? I had slept, hadn't I? I had slept *well* in fact. At least I think I had. I had remembered hearing noises the first night I had arrived but again, none of this now felt like it had really happened. Had I become so detached from reality that even in death I couldn't figure out what had been real or not since I arrived in Jersey. My eyes searched to find Carrie. She was still there, staring blankly at the recently dug hole, frozen. How could she see me, touch me, talk to me even if I was really dead? And if I wasn't, what the fuck was in the coffin and in the grave?

"Maybe we should open it up?" I blurted out.

"Open what up?" came the aggrieved reply.

"The coffin."

"There is no coffin, Nick."

"What do you mean there must be a ..."

"It's an empty grave."

"But ... but you said it was my grave?" I was gaining hope.

"Your tombstone is written, Nick, already written, and the soil has been dug."

"But I'm here. I'm *here*!"

"Are you really? Search your feelings, Nick, seriously. What the fuck is going on?" *Again, the same unanswerable question.*

"Maybe they thought I died, maybe I'm on a surgeons table somewhere, or in a coma, I don't know?"

But I did know. No one writes up an epitaph and sticks it on a tombstone if that person is still alive; not even my parents. I knew inside also. Something within me, telling me, maybe had always told me since ...

"You just haven't been buried yet." Carrie interrupted my awakening.

I shakily got to my feet and shuffled over to her. She no longer issued warnings for me to stay away. Her instant reaction to what was a ridiculous situation was again one of protection for me but now she was amiss with any answers.

I stared at the gravestone, saw the inscription for myself and as more tears rolled, I studied the fresh earth of where I was to be buried. Yet in all of this confusion something else did not feel right, as if there was something so obviously missing. I glanced backwards and forwards between the two areas that marked my own, personal charnel house and suddenly it dawned on me.

"There's no dates," I started, "no dates on my tombstone." I pointed to the gap which had so obviously been left vacant. "Why would they leave off the dates?"

"I really don't know? About any of this I really don't know."

Carrie grabbed my hand and instantly let go. Then she grabbed it again, over and over, before getting to her feet, where she pinched and pulled at me, slapping me across the face before looking at the redness it caused her own hand. Finally, and ever so tenderly, she kissed me.

"I'm all out of answers." Running her tongue over her own lips. "But you taste very real to me."

"I need to see my parents, surely then they'll realise that they've made a mistake. Someone has definitely made a mistake. I'm here, still alive, however much they want to pretend otherwise." I squashed deep down what I assumed to be so. There *was* hope after all.

I felt the blood rushing through my legs as the adrenaline kicked in and I was out of the graveyard and onto the path before turning and this time hurrying Carrie to come with me. I heard her whimper, but didn't wait ... couldn't wait ... for her.

The now familiar path seemed much shorter as I sprinted and leapt over any obstacle in the way, I reached the rise and dextrously manoeuvred up the abandoned tree roots, breathing heavily until I was eventually stopped in my tracks at the gravel driveway by the appearance of my mother and father huddled together. I called out after them and sprinted across the empty space between us before being briefly distracted by the tow bar on our car outside. My calls ebbed as I followed them into the dark, dust-filled humidity of the garage and witnessed that on top of a trailer there lay an open casket, containing a very pale version of myself.

"Dad, Dad?" No reply. "Dad...Mum, Mum. Please, it's not me, it's not. I'm not dead."

I angrily grasped at my mother as she leant over the coffin to kiss the intruder and at the same time, she shuddered as my hand went through her body.

I tried again and again to grab hold of her, turning to my father behind, asking for answers. He too was looking at the still body in the coffin and not directly at me, his son. In desperation I flung out my arms to shake him so he could feel I was very real and very warm, but as my body disappeared through his I stumbled against the side of the garage, instantly reacting to the bottle I had knocked off the shelf but was unable to catch. My mother jerked away from the body and looked at my father.

"Sorry dear," he said, "I'll clean that up in the morning ... after ..." Before he could finish, my mother was out of the garage. Her silhouette in the low sunlight took on a fairy-like deity and her footsteps quickly silenced. I turned back to my father who, whilst closing the coffin, was sobbing a goodbye; all too quickly he was also out of the garage letting peace fall once more.

Voices disturbed the brief moment of quiet and my head began to hurt from confusion and contradiction. Above all of this, the voice that shouted the loudest was of course Sophie's:

"I told you I'd win, Nick, I always do."

I stood and stared at the coffin whilst Sophie's uttering continued over and over again. Too many questions once more remained unanswered and the brief beginnings of a resolution to my failure with Sophie now took on an entirely different path.

I heard footsteps on the gravel.

"Nick? Nick are you in here?" Carrie's eyes squinted at me in the darkness.

"You were right. In a way we both were," I assessed.

Carrie stepped into the garage and first saw me before diverting her eyes to the coffin. She approached it cautiously.

"Don't." I said.

"Is it really?"

I nodded as I motioned towards Carrie, seizing her face, kissing her long and deep. Only when I pulled her into the descending light of the late afternoon, did she disconnect and turn her head away from the maple casket containing my body.

"Are your parents in?" I asked.

"What? Erm, no, the car's not outside."

"You've got a computer yeah? A laptop, tablet or something?"

"Yes, all three actually and an iPhone." She pulled one out of her pocket. "Have you not ..."

"That'll do. Look up 'Sophie Pemberton suicide'." I patted my pockets ... pointlessly.

"Nick I don't think ..."

"Look, Carrie, I've just had the freakiest last few hours so if you can please just do as I ask, I'd really fucking appreciate it right now."

Carrie's eyes welled up, "Nick, don't make me ..."

I snatched the phone off her, opened the browser and without having to type anything, the story of my death was on screen via *Facebook* as a RIP page.

"You ... you knew?" I queried.

"I stopped to look after we left the graveyard, you ran out of sight and I just ... I just checked to see."

"I'm not ... wasn't even ... on *Facebook*." I started. "Sophie asked me to come off it."

"Your friend set it up. *John?* It was a link from Google news."

135

I looked down at the names. All sending their condolences.

Nick - always a good friend, RIP buddy. This was John's, despite the fact that I *hadn't* been a good friend for the last couple of years.

Nick, the whole world was ahead of you, so sadly taken from us. Thomas and Heather Guest. My Uncle and Aunt.

Nick: a great writer, promising sportsman and a gentle soul. George Balston. My English teacher from Sage Green.

And there were numerous others.

I could sense Carrie tapping impatiently, fiddling with her hair, nails, teeth, fingers, anything to speed up my trauma. And finally, there it was:

My boyfriend, Nick. I will luv u 4ever - despite what you tried to do. Wish I had a shoulder to cry on. Sophie Pemberton :-(xxx

CHAPTER TWO
The Reckoning

We approached the unhinged, waist-high gate, resting against the small, crooked remains of a fence. The words Wolf's Lair *were faintly etched within the wood; a smear of deep red through the letters.*

"It's time for you to understand everything, Nick."

I had a sense of foreboding as I approached the doorway. Carrie pulled out a key and undid the out-of-place padlock and lifted the door whilst kicking repeatedly at the bottom. It edged forward a little at a time. I wasn't prepared for what greeted me inside; Sophie was sat at the table, her head bowed.

I shuddered at her heavily bulbous belly, protruding over her baggy, designer jeans. Yet she looked healthy, as on the day I first met her. She was whispering a nursery rhyme causing a small, blonde child in the chair opposite to giggle: "A pocket full of posies ... "

The floor creaked underfoot as I shifted my weight; and the nursery rhyme, along with the giggles, ceased. The girl was the first to look up at me. Her hair seemed darker than I first noticed and I could see my eyes in hers as she dropped something to the floor. I could make out the Walt Disney character Pluto on the child's knife for a brief second, before he vanished under droplets of blood. The girl held her wrists out towards me, extending her hands backwards to increase the flow. I looked to Sophie, who whilst stroking her tummy, had started the nursery rhyme once more, "Ring a ring a roses ... ". As she lifted her head and scowled at me, her appearance morphed. Her matted hair stuck to the sides of her ruddy face and she smiled, causing her blistered lips to crack and bleed. The rubbing of her pregnant stomach became more intense with the rising volume of the song. Over and over again, " ... atishoo atishoo, we all fall down ..." Until finally she picked up a kitchen knife and began hacking into her gut and unborn child.

I sunk to my knees, sobbing as I bent myself into my hands. Only when Carrie knelt down and put her arm around me did the nursery rhyme and the sound of puncturing flesh finally stop.

"Just like the pool, Nick, this place can help you." Carrie whispered.

This time there were no tears of childhood nostalgia but screams, my own screams that I had finally lost my sanity.

After a short while, I stopped rocking myself backwards and forward. I could feel Carrie's hand on my back, burning through me – getting hotter and hotter the longer I sobbed. I was conscious of how I had begun to look and gathered my thoughts as best I could and whilst doing so, the room emptied its ghosts.

"Better?" she asked rather coldly.

"Um, yeah, I guess?" I muttered.

"I'm sorry, Nick, I didn't think that would be so aggressive for you?"

She got up and walked into the room, sitting at the chair once occupied in my thoughts by Sophie.

"What is all of this?" I asked.

"You need to come to terms with what happened Nick." she started. "This place, whatever it is, helps you with the past."

"Who are you exactly?" I was bitter and felt hard done by. It was a game but only she was playing. It was like Sophie all over again.

"Don't think so much. You know what is true." Her stomach swelled and her lips cracked, "These ghosts will follow you wherever you go."

I flinched, yet I was no longer in the cottage. Instead I was outside the garage, its door now closed. Night had fallen and a small long-haired figure was knelt over me.

"Sophie? Sophie?"

"No, Nick, not Sophie."

As my vision cleared I saw Carrie looking down into her lap. She looked like a child as her bottom lip quivered.

"I'm sorry," I muttered. But the hurt was all too obvious. "I must have passed out or something?"

"I was worried you'd hit your head, but then ..."

"How much damage can a ghost do to himself right?"

"To other people, maybe you are causing pain? People that are trying to help you."

"Help me with what? Dying? The afterlife? How do you know it wasn't me that contributed to her demise and therefore being punished for it?"

"Because you're too giving Nick. Too appreciative of the world around you and the person you chose to date. You gave her everything. You let her have her space when she needed it and was always there for her when she needed you. That's what perfect boyfriends do!"

"Then why?"

"Sociopath Nick, she is a sociopath."

"*Was*."

"*Is* remember."

"What am I supposed to do, Carrie? I'm dead but still here. It's fucking limbo isn't it? For what reason exactly? To completely fuck me up by showing me the life I could've had? For reasons of justice whilst that fucking bitch lives on, getting away with whatever she got away with?"

"And what exactly did she get away with? And what exactly is your own justice?"

We stared at each other, daring one another to look away, until finally and at the same time agreed:

"Revenge."

For which Carrie added, "For else these ghosts will follow you wherever you go."

CHAPTER THREE

Sociopath

Sociopath *noun*

- *a person with a personality disorder manifesting itself in extreme antisocial attitudes and behaviour and a lack of conscience.*

Ref: http://www.oxforddictionaries.com/us/definition/american_english/sociopath

I had heard the term sociopath before but had never really investigated its meaning. Psychopaths are the term people seem keener to discuss, such is their standing in popular culture and the easily referable infamous names attached to them. Carrie had brought her *iPad* into the woods and we were sitting around the tree I had slept under when she had first introduced herself to me. As Carrie slowly began to scan the Internet, cursing at how crap her 4G connection was, she explained to me the differences between the two. We agreed that some of the defining boundaries crossed over and that some of the attributes are somewhat 'fuzzy'. Indeed it would also seem that some of those people labelled psychopaths were in fact sociopaths but neither were something to be proud of. As we argued the case for just how 'psycho' or 'socio' Sophie was, we found several 7-point guides and an extremely concise 11-point guide on the internet via the *Huffington Post* which flagged up personality traits of sociopathic people.

Carrie handed me a blue pen, with Jersey Tourism etched across it.

"Summer job last year," she shrugged, before prompting me to make extensive notes in reference to Sophie in the back of my unused diary, in order to fathom just what I/we were up against and settle the case once and for all for whom we were dealing with. I wrote down each flag, giving evidence underneath of Sophie's part to play in my assessment of her:

'Could that amazing new person you or a loved one is dating actually be a sociopath? It's not as far-fetched as you might imagine. Roughly one in 25 Americans is a sociopath, according to Harvard psychologist Dr. Martha Stout, author of The Sociopath Next Door.

Of course, not all sociopaths are dangerous criminals.
But they certainly can make life difficult, given that the
defining characteristic of sociopathy is antisocial
behaviour.'

Ref: http://www.huffingtonpost.com/2013/08/23/11-signs-dating-a-sociopath_n_3780417.html

Here are 11 RED FLAGS to look out for:

RED FLAG #1. Having an oversized ego.

*The Diagnostic and Statistical Manual of Mental
Disorders (DSM-V)* notes that sociopaths have an inflated
sense of self. They are narcissists to the extreme, with a
huge sense of entitlement, Dr. Seth Meyers, a clinical
psychologist with the L.A. County Department of Mental
Health, wrote for Psychology Today. They tend to blame
others for their own failures.

*Sophie: She always believed she could get anyone she wanted: be
it man or woman, any job she wanted and live any life she pleased. It was
always those around her who let her down and quashed her dreams by not
living up to her expectations.*

RED FLAG #2. Lying and exhibiting manipulative behaviour.

Sociopaths use deceit and manipulation on a regular basis. Why? "Lying for the sake of lying. Lying just to see whether you can trick people. And sometimes telling larger lies to get larger effects," Dr. Stout told *Interview Magazine*.

Sophie: This is the big one and involves the story that Sophie had told me on the very first date we had. This was the deal-breaker for me and it changed the way I saw her. It made me want to look after and protect her, forever. This was the information I have withheld from Carrie about Sophie but considering all that has happened and with my new perspective on Sophie, I needed to explain this fully to Carrie once we finished this note taking ...

RED FLAG #3. Exhibiting a lack of empathy.

"They don't really have the meaningful emotional inner worlds that most people have and perhaps because of that they can't really imagine or feel the emotional worlds of other people," commented M. E. Thomas, a diagnosed sociopath and author of *Confessions Of A Sociopath*. "It's very foreign to them."

145

Sophie: A complete lack of interest in the emotional distance I had with my family and the reasoning's behind why I counted on my close friends more than anyone. She was quick to take the latter from me and leave me as a loner with only her to depend on. She was only interested in my dreams if they fit in with hers and would use these to her advantage.

RED FLAG #4. Showing a lack of remorse or shame.

The DSM-V **entry on antisocial personality disorder indicates that sociopaths lack remorse, guilt or shame.**

Sophie: Would call me intermittently in the many times we had briefly broken up to ask for 'company'. She told me how at school, when she was fourteen, she seduced a teacher in his back office whilst there was a full class waiting for him in the very next room. As she walked through the classroom to disapproving looks, she 'spun' her knickers around one finger, whilst flicking the bird with the other to her fellow students. She told me she did it as the teacher was a sleaze and knew the word would get around school and he would be struck off, whilst she would be considered the poor innocent one. Sophie told me he had been subsequently jailed for it and had lost his family. She believed people should take more responsibility for their actions. She was also rather proud of the amount of partners she had had sex with - believing all to be infatuated with her.

RED FLAG #5. Staying eerily calm in scary or dangerous situations.

A sociopath might not be anxious following a car accident, for instance, M.E. Thomas said. And experiments have shown that while normal people show fear when they see disturbing images or are threatened with electric shocks, sociopaths tend not to.

Sophie: The incident with Pissy Pants in the Lunatic Asylum - one to hide from Carrie!

RED FLAG #6. Behaving irresponsibly or with extreme impulsivity.

Sociopaths bounce from goal to goal, and act on the spur of the moment, according to the *DSM*. They can be irresponsible when it comes to their finances and their obligations to other people.

Sophie: Also see RED FLAG #4. She had sudden urges to go to places to make out and want others to witness her doing so. She had a

147

guilty pleasure in wearing little to no underwear and making me (and others) very aware of it. She also owed me money - a lot of money.

RED FLAG #7. Having few friends.

Sociopaths tend not to have friends--not real ones, anyway. "Sociopaths don't want friends, unless they need them. Or all of their friends are superficially connected with them, friends by association," psychotherapist Ross Rosenberg, author of the *Human Magnet Syndrome*, told *The Huffington Post.*

Sophie: She picked up and dropped friends constantly. Using them as she did me. All of the friends she did appear close to were male. A constant reminder of this was via her Facebook profile.

RED FLAG #8. Being charming--but only superficially.

Sociopaths can be very charismatic and friendly -- because they know it will help them get what they want. "They are expert con artists and always have a secret agenda," Rosenberg said. "People are so amazed when they find that someone is a sociopath because they're so amazingly effective at blending in. They're masters of disguise. Their main tool to keep them from being discovered is a creation of an outer personality."

As M.E. Thomas described in a post for *Psychology Today*: "You would like me if you met me. I have the kind of smile that is common among television show characters and rare in real life, perfect in its sparkly teeth dimensions and ability to express pleasant invitation."

Sophie: Had the ability to seduce even the most unreceptive person. Within five minutes of meeting someone she would declare them her soul mate, and them likewise.

RED FLAG #9. Living by the "pleasure principle."

"If it feels good and they are able to avoid consequences, they will do it! They live their life in the fast lane -- to the extreme -- seeking stimulation, excitement and pleasure from wherever they can get it," Rosenberg wrote in *Human Magnet Syndrome*.

Sophie; Risk taking in public - sex, smoking, drugs etc. Always 'nicking' her dad's car. Always asking me to do her homework as she was too busy preparing for a night out (usually not with me).

RED FLAG #10. Showing disregard for societal norms.

They break rules and laws because they don't believe society's rules apply to them, psychiatrist Dr. Dale Archer wrote in a blog on *Psychology Today*.

Sophie: Ever since she could remember she told me she had never worn a bikini top whilst on holiday, regardless to what type of resort she was staying at and would openly walk through the hotel to the pool or beach without doing so. She was on her holidays after all. Once though, when she went to the Maldives with some relatives who had paid for her, she had been vilified by security for going topless and they were so out of order that she got the next flight home.

She would drive fast and without consideration for others - often jumping lights, driving whilst drunk or high. She also consistently skipped class to do more 'glamorous' activities, despite informing me that she had been.

RED FLAG #11. Having "intense" eyes.

Sociopaths have no problem with maintaining uninterrupted eye contact. "Our failure to look away politely is also perceived as being aggressive or seductive," M.E. Thomas wrote for *Psychology Today*.

Sophie: Always intense yet endearing, I was always the one to look away from her gaze first. She would hold her eyes to mine and it would melt me every time.

Further to this, I quickly realised that my assessment at the time that Sophie might have been bipolar was wrong, and indeed my very assumption of this only helped her continue with the lies and narcissistic behaviour, using this as reasoning behind some of her actions. Without me knowing, I was a puppet to her hand and I was thinking up ways to feed her sociopathic tendencies by finding things wrong with her - only fuelling her power over me. She knew I was onto something but took great delight all the same in agreeing with my assessments and making those symptoms her new reasoning's behind her behaviour. As long as I didn't uncover the truth, I was putty in her hands, she had indeed, played me until my last breath.

I looked at my answers to the flags raised and couldn't believe I had been so stupid; weak; gullible. Yes, towards the very end of our relationship, I had begun to realise things weren't as she had made them out to be and I was questioning her increasingly erratic behaviour and historical facts about her past, but in my melodramatic assessment of our relationship, I still believed it was me that had been the issue and the problem, such were her manipulative ways.

The tears that then flowed were ones of aggression and utter disgust of Sophie Pemberton. She had taken the last years of my life, turned me against my friends and distanced me further from my family. Not content with that, she had somehow ended my life whilst initiating her own fake suicide. I had already wasted enough time on us, now I had nothing to lose; it was time to end her.

"I need to find her." I said.

"I already have." Carrie handed me the *iPad*.

The headline was from a few days ago on the BBC Website:

'Girl Institutionalised Following Failed Suicide Pact'

CHAPTER FOUR
The Lunatic Asylum Part I - The Dare

The news article told how there had been an agreement between myself and Sophie in which we would end it together and help each other in doing so. But it also reported that there were irregularities in the story given by Sophie Pemberton. There were concerns that she might have been covering for me and that I had possibly tried to kill her, making it look like a suicide and that she, in defending herself, had fatally stabbed me.

I perused several other articles, each contradicting one another without any agreeing on what actually happened. Most of which were, surprise surprise, pure speculation. Doctor's reports confirmed that from the angle of the cuts inflicted on Sophie proved she must have done it to herself. It was also considered however, that I might have been behind her, overpowering her to slice the blade into her own arm. There was severe bruising to her wrists to back up this idea, although other articles believed I had done this to stem the blood-flow. One newspaper even believed that there might have been a third party involved as the police had interviewed a man in his mid twenties and another who was nearly fifty, both of which had been in contact regularly with her in the preceding few weeks; they had also spoken with a female counsellor.

The media were having a field day; Sophie hadn't talked since the incident and was now in full-time care at *St Dymphna's Hospital for the Insane*, close to where she lived. *The Lunatic Asylum* as it was known since I was a kid, was shut down in the 1970s due to abuse of patients and several unauthorised experiments. The large block building with tall windows housing chequered white wooden frames enclosed by narrow, rusted bars and was built in the Victorian era. The draconian care administered suited this monstrosity perfectly. When times were hard after the stock market crash in 2007 and recession took place, many more people were in need of care and *The Asylum* reopened. I couldn't think of a more apt place for Sophie to reside.

"What is it, Nick?" Carrie asked.

"I know this place, it used to scare the hell out of us as kids. We would dare each other to go in there at night, on our own, whilst the rest of the group would hang back at the entrance. We would use a screwdriver and chisel off the door numbers in sequence to prove how far we got. They were like trophies. Each subsequent night the next in line would have to get the next one, therefore we would end up deeper and deeper inside ... *The Asylum*."

"Sounds like the sort of thing kids do all the time, only nowadays they would *FaceTime* the whole process."

"We weren't allowed our mobiles with us, that was deemed too chicken shit. That place scared the fuck out of me - out of all of us."

"Yeah but it's just a hospital right, there are dozens of them up and down the country."

I put a hand on Carrie's knee, squeezing slightly; I would have to tell her after all.

"One boy from the year below us, a large fat boy called ... umm ... shit what was his *name*? Well he was in remedial class for all of his subjects and had dropped down a few years. I think he actually might have been eighteen. Anyway he went missing in there."

"Are you sure that's not an urban myth? These ... "

155

I gripped harder. "No he went in and never came out. God what *was* his name?!"

"Just tell the story."

"Okay, okay. His sister was in our year, she hated him, she wanted to be, you know, one of those *cool* kids but he was always following her: trying to sit with her at lunch and make conversation with her in the corridors. She would yell at him, scream until she was literally spitting at him until he would wet himself in front of the whole school. Being cool, was much more important than looking after your 'slow' brother. *Paul!* That was it! *Paul Pissed his Pants!* This quickly became *Pissy Pants Paul* and then just plain *Pissy Pants*."

"But how did he end up in there? In the hospital? Could his parents not look after him?"

"He didn't go in as a patient."

Carrie looked startled, "What are you telling me?"

"It was the cool kids that started it. They told his sister that if she wanted to be 'accepted' she would have to provide them with more amusement than just making her brother piss himself.

One day after school, just before we broke up for Christmas, she offered to walk home with Pissy Pa ... with Paul. He was so delighted that his sister was being his friend that he'd failed to notice the ever growing group behind him as they walked the short-cut home, past *The Asylum*."

I twitched. It wasn't a story I had wanted to tell.

"His sister had walked him around the back of the building, and when the group followed, Piss ... sorry ... Paul turned and looked at them all with a look of trepidation, and realisation. He was slow but he wasn't stupid. He just had one of those learning disorders which seems to affect every other person nowadays."

Carrie sat back, fiddling with her blue pen until it broke apart and spewed its contents onto the ground.

"He just needed to get one room number, that was all. Yet that wasn't *all*. Every single room number had *already* been taken."

"So he was getting sent in there whilst everyone knew full well he could not get a number?"

"Not exactly."

"What do you mean not exactly?"

"The ground floor had been emptied of numbers yeah but the second floor, the floor where the experiments had taken place ... well ... no one had ever dared to go up there."

"And Paul did?"

"No one knows for sure."

"What do you mean?"

I had tears in my eyes.

"What are you saying, Nick?"

"He was singing as he entered *The Asylum*. Everyone thought that was hilarious and Paul seemed to think people were laughing with him, not at him. God I'll never forget that song."

I gnawed at my thumb scar causing it to bleed. "He sang 'number fell down' at every door until we could barely hear him. He then shouted, 'No more doors, no more doors, Sis!'

With a big smile she turned around to us all, 'Try upstairs Pauly, make me proud and get me a number'. His singing muffled further and then there was silence."

I went for the thumb again, sucking on the raw skin.

"Everyone began to look at each other, most were nervously giggling, but his sister wasn't. She looked annoyed, irritated. Quietly she started, ever so softly: 'Pissy Pants Pauly, Pissy Pants, Pissy Pants'. Over and over, getting louder and louder. A couple of people mouthed the words before thinking better of it, and then one by one, people began leaving. I pulled at her, trying to get her to stop, a couple of us did, but without looking away from the entrance she battered us away.

158

'Pissy Pants, hurry up you fucking retard, everyone's leaving'. But then we were all stopped in our tracks. Every single person turned in unison to the one single noise that came from within the asylum: a low, bellowing wail. The gasps coming from the group were only interrupted when his sister waltzed through us, giggling to herself."

I looked at Carrie and then to my feet, dusting a leaf away from them.

"He ... he what exactly? He died?" Carrie backed away from me.

"I was the first in, followed quickly by John. We used the torches on our phones to light up the long hallway. Several of us were now in the building, bunched up and slowly moving forwards as a pack. We reached the bend which signalled the end of the ground floor rooms, and all too soon we saw him; laying at the foot of the stairwell, his glazed eyes fixated on the hanging corpse at the top of the landing."

"Oh my God, Nick that's horrific." Carrie leaned over and it was her turn to grip me.

"I tried ... we ... we tried to resuscitate him but he was already cold. In the flashlights he looked deathly pale ... ghostly."

"And the hanging ... ?"

"A girl from school who had gone missing. Her mum had worked in the asylum and it turns out that she had been cyber-bullied about it in the weeks leading up to her suicide. Paul must have seen her and it literally scared him to death. It was reported he had a heart defect but none of us bought that, not really, although I guess that does make sense now."

"That's so, so sad." Carrie said. She had tears running down her cheeks and was the same colour that Paul had been, the last time I saw him there, laying at the bottom of the stairs. "But why tell me the story, Nick? What does it have to do with anything?"

"Sophie was Paul's sister." I confessed.

.   .   .

We sat still for a while, unable to look each other in the eye. Finally she piped up.

"So you knew Sophie at this point? Was this before or after The Ball?"

"It was before, but only a year tops." Carrie's eyes bore into me. "I didn't know it was her, I swear I never put two and two together. Paul was simply *Pissy Pants Paul*, I never knew his surname."

160

"But surely you recognised her, knew at *The Ball* she was the same girl that had ... that had sold out her brother. Jesus, Nick she pretty much sent him to his death."

"It wasn't her fault, really it wasn't. Just a stupid prank that went wrong. If that girl hadn't hung herself well then ... Paul would still be here. Sophie panicked and just ran, that's what I thought – we all did. She was in shock, so much so, and for so long, that she never brought it up when we were together."

"But when you saw her at *The Ball* you said you'd never seen her before, that she was an instant attraction – *love at first sight* no?"

"Yes, yes all of those things. But in that time she had changed schools. Besides, Sophie had this uncanny ability to look so very different in the way she presented herself, her hair colour, make up, clothing – even her whole demeanour. It was like she was many different people."

"She kept reinventing herself. Is that what you're trying to say?"

"I guess that's exactly what I'm saying."

"And everyone fell for it?" Carrie stated. "What the hell was she doing at *The Ball* anyway? So soon after her brother's death?"

"It *had* been a year, or there abouts."

"Yes but those people who had been there when she encouraged Paul into the hospital: they would also have been at *The Ball!* Anyone else surely would have kept away - been ashamed; culpable; remorseful."

"She was the centre of attention and people were rallying around her, I never realised why until ... well, until it was too late ... and I'd fallen for her."

"How convenient this all sounds." Carrie stated again and on seeing me squirm, "Don't worry, Nick, you're not the first and you certainly won't be the last to fall for such a person, although I'll never understand how you didn't see the warning signs."

"I know, I know and that's what's so fucking frustrating. She wasn't ... shouldn't have been the one. Things didn't match up in her timeline of the things she had told me. I sussed that out but when I tried to dig deeper; to get answers; to get the truth; she ran away from me and to someone else."

"It sounds as if you have a fair idea of all the answers you seek." Not quite a statement or a question.

"I just wanted to hear her explanation so that I wouldn't have to make them up in my own mind. For the longer we stayed together, the worse my own answers became and I didn't want those answers to be the real ones, I wanted her to tell me something else; something which proved that I'd got it all wrong."

"You're losing me."

"Will you come with me?" I pleaded. Carrie didn't need to ask where. "On the way I'll tell you why."

"Why what, Nick?"

"Why I got sucked in and why I stayed with her."

"You fell in love, isn't that it? Isn't that enough."

"Maybe," I replied, "but there was more to it than that; much more."

CHAPTER FIVE

Falling in Love

Carrie booked tickets for the boat online, automatically selecting two passengers. We looked at each other, saying nothing, before she clicked to confirm. She had also booked her parents' car onto the boat. This excited, yet concerned me.

"Well how else are we going to get there?"

"I take it you have a license then?"

"A provisional. Besides you have to be over 25 to be able to take a car on the ferry."

"So how ...?"

"I'll borrow my mum's license. I look a lot like her and I'll just wear some older clothes and make-up, flatten down my hair. Nick, don't look so worried."

I shrugged my shoulders. It was obvious we had no other way.

She pulled the license out from her purse and smiled at me reassuringly. I couldn't help but laugh awkwardly.

I ran out from the woods and across the courtyard to pack a bag. We only had an hour before we needed to get to the boat and in the failing summer light we knew there could be some serious traffic as people flocked off the beaches. The ferry we booked was the slow overnighter but it was the one chance we had to take the car before Carrie's parents raised the alarm. She was going to leave them a note, telling them not to worry and was very blasé about deceiving them - I got the impression it wasn't the first time.

"Sometimes the wrong things need to be done, for the right things to be achieved." Carrie had told me in front of her house.

I stuffed a light rucksack with a change of underwear and just before leaving the house I went back to my bedroom and grabbed a jumper, tying it around my waist. In the doorway between my room and the landing I stopped and considered the stairs below me before looking back over my shoulder. Everything in the room looked the same - familiar but of no comfort. The baby blue pillows and duvet didn't *sit* right anymore. The jeans folded neatly in the wardrobe alongside meticulously ironed shirts - the garments of a

165

stranger. *Dead man's clothes.* I shuddered in the disbelief that on my return I was unlikely to be able to change anything. I blocked out the voices but believed them when they told me it was time to say '*Goodbye*'.

I heard the car start up outside and the lower part of the house lit up in a wash of light before quickly falling into darkness once more. I flicked off the switch on the bedroom wall and pulled the door closed without looking back. The image I had of me laying on top of the bed, slowly turning the sheets from baby blue to deep red caused me to hurriedly depart, descend the stairs, and out of the front door, not bothering to lock it behind me. This was Jersey after all I told myself - bringing no comfort whatsoever.

I crouched to confirm the driver before throwing my bag in the back and getting in the passenger seat up front. Carrie was true to her word and wearing thick foundation with burgundy lipstick and blue eye shadow. I'm not quite sure if it really made much difference but she wore a silk scarf and sunglasses in her hair, which was now quite curly. There were streaks of grey at the roots.

"Model paint. Works every time!" She was obviously very pleased with herself. "If you didn't know who I was, Nick you would think I was at least forty-years-old right?

"Yeah sure, it's really good." I lied.

Traffic was manageable on the way to the port. The light had faded more rapidly than expected and again the air was clammy. We were directed to queue with dozens of other cars, all vying for one of the two ticket booths where our passports and documents would be checked. I looked around me to see if anyone was aware of my presence but it was too dark to gauge any kind of reaction. I felt like getting out of the car and screaming, just to put my own mind at rest, but thought better of it. As we inched ever nearer to the small huts, containing customs officers our already minimal conversation dried up completely and Carrie stalled the car twice before we finally pulled up to the window of the booth and handed over the e-tickets shown on the *iPad* screen.

"You lose someone on the way?" said the stout female officer behind the desk. She was wearing an ill-fitting white shirt that showed off every bump and a black tie, which was stained with something crusty. Carrie looked at me. "You booked two tickets." said the woman.

"Err...yeah sorry, my neighbour was taken ill." Carrie informed her.

"You might be able to get that back on insurance?" She smiled pointing at the fare, "Just make sure they get a note from the Doctor, although it's probably cheaper if they didn't bother." She raised her eyebrows.

"Okay, thank you, will do."

"Hmm ... okay. Please queue in row six, have a safe trip."

As Carrie drove on I couldn't help but notice a second woman in the booth, a woman who wasn't in uniform but who had placed a hand on the officer's shoulder and whispered something in her ear just as we pulled away, never once dropping eye contact with me.

A short while later, we were waved through and onto the boat. Deck hands directed the parking and we were so tightly against other cars that I couldn't get out my side. I noticed that other passengers had been encouraged out of their cars prior to parking up.

"I might just stay in the car." I said.

"I'll go and get us some food and come back down." Carrie agreed.

"I'm not sure you're allowed down here once the boat gets going?"

"Well you're down here!"

"Yes but apparently I'm not noticeable."

"They won't notice me either, I'll be discreet."

"Seriously, you don't have to for my sake."

"What's the option? Sleeping in the canteen with a hundred other people? In case you hadn't noticed I didn't get us a cabin."

"Thanks, Carrie." I was really touched that she would risk further trouble for herself.

"There are blankets in the boot. Fold the back seats down and we pretty much have a bed." She kissed my cheek and was encouraged out of the car by the steward who was far too busy getting irate at people's parking attempts to question an interaction between a teenager and her 'imaginary friend'. Carrie gave me a considerate glance and then she was gone, lost amongst the stressed travellers at the bottom of the stairs, which led to the main deck.

I was keen at the thought of me and Carrie spending the nine-hour journey here, in the back of the car, together and alone. I hopped onto the back seats and felt around them until I found something that seemed like a lever. Pulling this, I struggled to hold the two seats that fell forward. Once down, I moved onto these and pulled another handle that dropped the last remaining seat and assessed our bedding area. It was a decent, larger than average vehicle, but it would still be a squeeze with the two of us lying down in the back. The seats also didn't lie flat so we'd be at a bit on an angle, which annoyed me somewhat and I was also frustrated that the sunroof wouldn't offer a view of the stars.

Could've got a better room, Nick.

An hour passed and it began to dawn on me that Carrie might not be able to come back after all. I hadn't seen anyone on the car deck since a few minutes after the boat had set sail, not even staff. I had laid the blankets out and to avoid creasing them, stayed seated in the front passenger seat. I looked at the refection of myself, first in the windows of the car, then the sun visor mirror and finally in the windows of other cars. All sent back perfectly normal images as if I were alive. I could perhaps understand it if I didn't have interaction with anyone, but Carrie, she had always seen me since coming to Jersey. Had always interacted with me and not just through voice or sight either; we had physically interacted. None of this made sense.

Knock, knock, knock.

I jumped in my seat and then looked for somewhere to hide.

"Nick open up. Quick, it's me."

"Yes, right, sorry." I leant across and clicked the central locking system. Carrie had two baguettes under her arm and a

170

couple of hot drinks in a cardboard holder in her other hand. I pushed the door out to help her and waited for the alarm to sound as it hit the adjacent car. We both stopped moving, but nothing.

"Fuck, Nick you almost blew our cover." There were other passengers towards the bow of the boat and I could feel the noise of the ships engines reduce to a purr.

"Sorry, I thought you weren't coming? Hang on? How are we here already?"

"It's Guernsey. We stop here on the way. It was the only time they unlocked the doors to the lower deck. Sorry, I did try to get down here sooner, pretending I'd left something in the car but they insisted they come down with me, so I just made an excuse that it really wasn't so important." She was excitable, that much was obvious. "This is fun!" Confirmation given.

"There's some stewards, you're going to have to hide." I pointed to the blankets in the back. Carrie nipped over the front seat, rubbing against me as she did and knocking the sunglasses off her head. She settled under the covers, but her giggles continued.

Shhh!" I said, "One's coming." But although she was quieter, she was still shaking. With the staff member only one

171

car away I quickly jumped into the back and clamped myself on top of her, holding her tightly, restricting her movement as much as I could. The deck hand's torchlight scanned the inside of the vehicle, hitting me directly in the eyes, causing me to shy away. When I looked back, he was gone.

I waited a few more minutes before I reluctantly removed myself off her. She was red-faced and still smiling when she finally appeared from under the covers.

"Sandwich?" she giggled, thrusting a baguette towards me. I took it from her but placed it up front, on the dashboard of the car. I lay back down, dragging the covers over me this time. Carrie unwrapped the cling-film from her sandwich and took a huge bite.

"It's better than it looks." she said, her mouth overflowing.

"Thanks but I think I'll wait until the other side."

"Are you queasy?"

"No, not really, well not from the boat anyway."

"It might be the fumes down here?"

"No, not the fumes either."

Carrie took one last enormous bite and then rewrapped the rest of her roll.

"You ready to tell me then?" she asked.

I sat back up, and in the rear of the car I stretched out as much as I could, horizontally. Carrie imitated my position, sitting herself aside yet facing me. I could see streaks of condensation glistening in the window behind her, but thankfully her face was shrouded in the ever-decaying light.

"The first time me and Sophie went on a date, I found it hard to engage with her at first. She was wearing a roll-neck top with a perfume brand written across it in large letters. We went to the cinema and saw the anniversary edition of Back to the Future, something she confessed she'd never seen. Within ten minutes of the film beginning though, she started acting up."

"Nick, can we go to those seats at the back?" Sophie asked.

"Yeah sure, if you're not comfy?" I looked behind me and saw the entire back row was free. Given the distance from the screen, it wasn't surprising.

"Too many people here," she whispered, before grabbing her bag and shuffling past those in the seats between the aisle and us. I noticed the uneaten popcorn she asked for at reception was still in its holder in the chair, before looking up to see her mouth something to an older guy in the aisle seat. I stumbled out behind her as quick as I could and followed her

up to the back seats, which were actually couple's couches. I smiled wryly, yet wasn't surprised I hadn't noticed them before.

We settled down together and she took off her jumper, revealing a crop top underneath. She placed the jumper so that it covered both of our laps and instantly ran her hand down, inside and between my legs. I could see the man on the end of the row below sneak a look back at Sophie, before catching my eye and jerking back towards the screen.

Sophie then started kissing my neck, making an ever so quiet humming noise that got louder as she pulled my hand towards her and between her legs. She flicked at one of the straps from her top so that it fell off her shoulder, revealing no bra underneath. Even in the dull light of the cinema screen, I could see her nipples were as hard as I was myself. We kissed heavily, long and deep as she half-turned towards me, draping her right leg over mine. Slowly she started to grind on my leg, pulling her arm out of top so that her left breast was now fully exposed. I avidly grabbed at it with my right hand and as soon as I had done, I came in my jeans. As she turned away from me to look back at the screen, I felt her breathing get even heavier before she also gave a low grunt. Within a few seconds she was fixing herself, removing her crop top to fully expose herself before casually putting it back on and pulling the jumper off us. I quickly put my hand to my groin, even in this light, I was obvious.

"Let's go, I'm bored of this movie," she said abruptly, before motioning me to walk in front of her.

174

As I left the cinema, I held the door open for her, only then did I realise she was a few seconds behind me. I guessed she must have needed to fix her clothing a little longer than I had realised.

When we were outside she asked, "Did you not want me?"

"It's a bit ... "

"This **is** a date, Nick. Or isn't it? Are you just leading me on?"

"Yes, a date but I've never really ... "

"So you didn't want me?"

"I thought we just did what you ... "

"Wanted? No. If you weren't going to fuck me I hoped you would have at least fingered me. It's not all about you, Nick."

"I'm sorry, I thought you had fun too, no?"

"Not properly no, not like you. You're just like all the other men."

"What do you mean all the other men?"

"Just wanting to please yourself, satisfy yourself, not giving a shit about how you go about doing that."

"I'm sorry, I didn't realise. I thought it was what you wanted. You did start it."

"What, not like you didn't want to? You need to be more caring, Nick, I'm not a piece of meat."

"But it was you that started it."

"I was giving you what you wanted."

"Sorry, I guess we got our wires crossed somewhere, I'm confused as to what I was supposed to do? I've never ... "

"You've never what? Done it? Yeah bullshit. You took full advantage. Trying to prove your worth in front of that guy in there." She began to storm off, pacing several yards ahead of me.

"Sophie, wait, I have no idea who that guy was."

She stopped, "Yeah well he kept looking at us."

"Well I guess it was kind of obvious what we were up to."

"Only if you're a bloke. Just treat me with more respect ok. And learn fast, I deserve to have as much fun as you."

"Okay sure I promise." I said. I was squinting, looking at the sky. How had things turned so sour so quickly?

"Sorry." she said, "It's probably not you, it's me. I just don't trust guys. I was raped a few years back." Sophie walked a few yards away from me and then stopped. She half looked back over her shoulder.

I accepted the invitation and came behind her, pulling her close to me. She was tense. Her rigid arms were folded across her chest.

"I'm so sorry," I said, "are you okay?" I pleaded.

She relaxed, turned around and embraced me tenderly. As she did, she whispered in my ear, "Just love me, Nick, that's all I ask."

"In that moment I did - and never stopped." I said.

"So then what happened?"

"I spent the night with her and I tried to make it all better, by ... well you know. I just wanted her to be aware that whatever had happened to her, whatever past life she had, that none of that mattered and I would be there to help her through it." I reddened.

Carrie, bit her upper lip and looked past me.

Finally, barely audible she whispered, "So *who* raped her?"

"She never really said. Just someone her father knew - one of his 'acquaintances'. Someone they were in business with."

"So what happened to him? Did he go down for it?"

"She said that no-one believed her. Her younger brother, the one that died, had walked in on them; interrupting. The boy had run to tell her father but by the time he came, the man had finished the job and Sophie was putting her clothes back on."

"So the man was still there when her father arrived?"

"Yeah, made a joke of it apparently – something along the lines of proving she wasn't a virgin. Whenever I asked Sophie about it, she'd clam up. At first I thought the man had taken her virginity at the same time as raping her, but towards the end, of us, she said she had messed around with a boy from school prior to any of this happening. I was grateful for that small mercy, even though that would have made her all the younger when she first ... "

Carrie interrupted, "Just how old was she when she was raped?"

"Twelve." I said instinctively.

"Fuck!"

"Bad huh?"

"So she never reported him?"

"No, she told her dad to do so apparently, and her dad had merely shrugged his shoulders, saying that she looked fine when he had seen her."

"But what was her response to that, I mean she would have been in shock, she must have been petrified. Were there marks? There's always marks, Nick, bruising you know, down there."

"She did say she was in shock, but that her dad must have felt guilty about it as he bought her a new iPod a short while afterwards."

"Fuck, what kind of family does that?"

"Sophie's." I stated.

"Now I'm beginning to realise why, Nick."

"Why?"

178

"Why you fell for her; felt you had to protect her; why you dropped everything for her and ..."

"Go on" I ask.

"Why maybe, you made a suicide pact with her, just like the papers say."

I thought quietly but within seconds I had my answer. "I just don't see me doing that? I would have tried everything to help her. Suicide wouldn't have been an option."

"Maybe you did try everything and maybe it did become an option; the only option."

"But in my memory that wasn't how it was. Sophie had run into the kitchen and started cutting herself; there was no pact, no agreement, no other knife. Surely if we made a pact we would have done it at the same time."

"But look at the outcome, Nick; apparently you're dead and she isn't. Explain that one."

"I can't." I said. "I can't explain any of this."

Fresh tears from both of us flowed and Carrie pulled me closer to her under the covers. We were both exhausted, frustrated, confused. I nestled my face into the nape of her neck. Shortly after, Carrie fell still and her breathing became heavier. I could feel the warm air on the top of my head and for a little while they starved off the dozens of voices in my head:

Loser. Coward. Rapist. Murderer.

.   .   .

I felt my back jolt. Opening my eyes I could see light streaming in through the moisture free car windows ... and we were moving.

"You awake, Nick?" Carrie asked, eyeballing me through the rear-view mirror from her driver's seat.

"Obviously!" I squinted back at her.

"Come up from there then, quickly, you need to direct me from here on in."

I stumbled into the front passenger seat. "We've got several hours before ... " I stopped in my tracks. "Wasn't that Cobb's Playing Field?" I said to nobody in particular.

"You tell me? We can't be far? Visiting times close at 6pm. We have an hour to do this."

"Jesus, how long?"

"You were well out of it, so I just left you to it, I was going to find a place to pull over just as you woke up. You must be starving? That baguette is still there, although I ate some. Which way now?"

"Err, straight through the roundabout, as long as you keep heading up you're fine."

"Are we close?" she asked.

"Twenty minutes that's all. I can't get over we're really here." I suddenly felt sick as we drove through the town and out the other side, to the residential district. I rewrapped the baguette without taking a bite.

"Take a left here, quick, here." I demanded.

Leaving no time to indicate, Carrie turned the car. "Now next right, then right again, then left and keep going up."

"But we've just ... " she paused, "what was down that street Nick?"

CHAPTER SIX

The Lunatic Asylum Part II - Sophie

"We're not far now." I said, trying to clear my head from the last several hours that I had missed. To be transported here so unprepared, I wanted delays, lots of them. "Maybe we should hold off until morning?"

"No, Nick. The boat is back first thing tomorrow morning. It's now or never. If you want me with you that is?"

"But it's getting too..."

"We still have half an hour."

"That's not long enough..."

"Too late."

The road finally gave way to a fork at its peak. On the main route it continued down, along its windy path through more trees. The *'To All Directions'* sign firmly pointing straight. Underneath this was the lighter coloured, newer signpost that pointed right: St Dymphna's Hospital. As Carrie pulled over and onto the dusty path the signage became more visible and someone had scribbled underneath *'The Assilum'*.

"Just kids, Nick. Whatever your thoughts or memories are of this place, that's not how it'll be now. They're all on medication to keep them in check. You know that right?"

But Carrie's words offered no comfort. I couldn't fathom how a mental hospital could ever be considered a serene place. Mad men; mad women; *crazies*. All shouting and screaming and trying to kill themselves or each other whilst masturbating in their own shit. The closest thing to hell on earth. One step before the ride down the River Styx and into the jaws of The Devil's charnel house, where more untold horrors lie. And how apt, that Sophie lyes here: ready for me; her; us; to be sent on that riverboat. There had to be more, there had to be another way.

Too late

We were greeted outside as soon as we got out of the car.

"Closing time is in a few minutes, you'll have to come back another ... " started a portly lady, ill-fitting glasses falling off the edge of her nose, her accent: thick Yorkshire. She smelt of bleach.

"Please, we've driven a very long way ... and besides, we have twenty minutes." Carrie was both firm and pleading.

The lady took off her glasses, bending the left arm straight before putting them back on. They were now closer to her eyes. She studied the front of the car, "It's very close to feeding time..."

"Please." Carrie was now in a submissive pose. Yet I had taken a step back towards the vehicle.

The woman looked at me, and I looked away. From that distance I was unsure if she was aware of me and if she was, my shaking.

Feeding time?

"Who?" she asked.

"Sophie," said Carrie

"Sophie Pemberton," I finally found my voice.

"Sophie Pemberton, confirmed Carrie."

"Okaaay ... you family?" She tilted her head.

"No, I'm a friend." Carrie started, "From school."

"You're accent's kinda funny?"

"I was only there for a couple of years before moving back home."

"That a Jersey plate?" asked the nurse.

Our twenty minutes were rapidly becoming fifteen.

"Yes, you've been?"

"Went every year for my wedding anniversary, until...well, Dennis passed."

"I'm sorry," said Carrie. Both were now looking at their feet. "I work for Jersey Tourism," she lied.

"Really? Hmm okay. I know how far you've come and because you're not family, you can have half an hour. You might be good for her." She began leading Carrie through the corridors, unlocking and locking several large barred doors painted grey to match the skirting boards. The rest was painted white. White ceilings, white floors, white walls; limited and simple furniture: white. We encountered a couple of other interns, most were gathered around a computer, others were hurriedly about the corridors and finally, one was mopping a floor; only this floor was not currently white.

"Ask about the family." I said, running my tongue around my gums.

"What about the family?" Carrie turned to me.

"Disgusting lot." The woman spoke up. "The things they did to her. Of course they deny everything and say that Sophie is delusional and should've been sectioned years ago. But sometimes when you look into a girl's soul you know she's telling the truth."

185

It was then that I doubted everything. Every little hint of progress I had made since meeting Carrie, now dissipated. This woman had interacted with Sophie. Treated her. Listened to her. Comforted her. All since the incident happened.

We walked along the corridor and eventually the stairs came into view. I held Carrie's sweaty hand.

"You're shaking," she whispered. Before following my gaze and she began to tremble too.

As we climbed the stairs I did all could to keep staring at my feet. Seeing *others* in limbo right now would be too much to bear. We turned left at the top and walked another long corridor to the furthest door at the end and to our right.

"Ask her about me." I murmured.

"Do know about the incident with Nick?"

The woman stopped fidgeting with the ring of keys and looked Carrie up and down.

"Oh yes, we all know about *him*. God forgive me, but thank the Lord he killed himself before I got my hands on him. He made his journey to hell before I or someone else could send him there. He was even worse than the family."

Carrie was twitching. If I could be heard, I would have shouted; screamed at this woman for the truth; for what Sophie had said; for the knowledge of what *I* had done.

"I knew Nick from school, he seemed like a nice guy."
Carrie spoke up.

Appreciated.

"They always do; the psychopaths; they always do. Who makes a suicide pack with a girl who's carrying his baby and then starts to cut her open instead of sticking to his part of the deal." The cell door is hastily unlocked. "She's inside and you have ten minutes, then I want you out of here. You're not family, you've made that clear but I don't think you're her friend either?" She looked Carrie eye, judging. "I'm only allowing you in because ... well, the Jersey thing. When the screaming starts, your visit is over."

.   .   .

Carrie stopped at the doorway to look at me: waiting, offering. The room was bleak. A solitary window, no more than a foot square, was opposite and easterly facing. There were two, pointless parallel bars, slightly rusted in the frame which housed no curtain nor blind. Carrie edged me, heels first, into the room. I was aware of the silhouette to my right: head sunken, arms wrapped about itself, perched at the edge of a dirty white, PVC covered bed. A single shackle into the wall, which split towards its back. The figure's hair indistinguishable for it lay, wet against its head. The black, scruffy style covered its whole face lest the lips. Cracked, blood red lips. There was nothing else in the room. The door shut behind us and I jumped as it locked and the shutter pulled to a close. The stink; the cold; the damp. This place seemed like a distant dream - one too real. In forty years, it simply hadn't changed.

"I wondered when you would show up." Sophie lifted her head. Her hair parted slightly to make out a dark, crusty nostril and one swollen eye which bore into me. Her eyes twitched to Carrie, "And I see you've brought the cavalry." I backed up against the wall as her gaze turned to me. "How's heaven, Nick? Oh not made it there yet? So then, how's your hell?"

"Look, he just wants to know what happened and then we'll go okay?" Carrie didn't sound like Carrie.

"I'll deal with you later bitch, what right do you have bringing him here?"

"He wanted, he, he needed to come." Still not sounding like Carrie.

"Bullshit. He's a gutless little cry baby. A pathetic little law-abiding, preachy, homiletic cunt."

188

"Where did you learn a word like that?" I was jolted into action.

"You used to like me using that word, Nick, don't you remember? I used to invite you into it."

"That's not the word I was referring…"

"Oh being in here has taught me a whole load of things. Tell me, Nick. What is it like being dead?"

Me and Sophie had interacted without a blink of an eye. The vile insults coming from her mouth a refreshing change from being ignored.

"You do know you're dead? Ha-ha wouldn't it be funny if poor little Nick thought he had gotten the better of me," she whispered to Carrie whilst taking a quick glance at the door.

"We're dealing with that," Carrie replied.

"Oh I don't think you are, Deary. Look at his little face, his poor little cute face. How he sulks, how he always sulked when he didn't get his own way with me."

"What own way?" I repulsed. She could fire her spat with me but not Carrie, this wasn't fair on her. "I only tried to help … "

"Help a girl that didn't need helping? I never asked … "

189

But it was now my turn to interrupt. "You did ask, many a time. You even went to counselling."

"I fucked the counsellor, that helped a great deal."

"What?"

"Yes, we chatted, she realised that I wasn't the problem and when I started to cry, so did she. She'll deny it of course, just like the teacher did but we did it alright; she came a great deal; we both did," she flicked her hair back and ran her eyes over Carrie as she protruded her tongue over her lips. Carrie looked away, down at the floor. My heart was beating ever faster.

"Stop it!" I implored.

"Stop what? Oh come on, Nick, you know I like to play these games; it's what first drove you to me. Remember the one I played with my brother?"

"Of course I remember."

"Well you never knew the reason why."

"You wanted to fit in, that's why."

"Oh no, he was the one that fitted in me. And his baby too."

"Surely not," enquired Carrie.

"Of course I aborted the thing, you remember don't you? I couldn't have risked a disgusting little mongrel, with a big moon face growing inside me - using me as a place of comfort. Disgusting creatures they are. Vile. No not a chance."

"She's just conjuring, Nick. Trying to hurt you."

"I said shut up you whore, can't you see me and Nick are having a conversation, one you're not invited to."

"She's messing with you, Nick, please."

"I'm not so sure she is. She did tell me she once had an abortion."

"Don't let her into your head again."

I looked at Carrie and then back at Sophie, before the latter spoke calmly:

"You never could tell what was real and what wasn't could you? You were my toy, my little play thing. How much money did you spend on me? How many friends did you lose over me? How many times did I fuck people behind your back just to get my kicks? *Tinder* is a wonderful app."

I trembled.

"Oh, Nick don't start with those tears again. You know I can't stand pathetic little cry babies."

I wiped away moisture from both eyes and on inspecting my fingers, expected more. *Pathetic* maybe, but *cry baby* no longer.

"Nothing shocks me with you anymore," I vented, "the guys ... and girls you used, the games you played with me and everyone else, all to get an easy ride."

"Now you're getting it! Come on. More. You're on a role!"

"And then there was the rape story," I finally said it.

Silence.

"Made up, to make people feel sorry for you." I continued.

"It wasn't made-up you little shit, when I was eleven I was raped by my brother."

"I thought you were twelve and he was a friend of your dad's?"

"*Whatever.* How do you expect my memory to be after being in here for so long?"

"Your memory was never that great, if you're going to lie at least be consistent.

"They beat me you know ... head trauma ... that causes ... mistakes ... memory loss. Don't be dumb."

"That was your downfall, that is how I found you out and that is why I became so messed up."

"And that is why you tried to kill me?" Her eyes cut into me, there was absolutely no shame in them whatsoever.

"Really?" I asked, "Is that what happened?"

Sophie looked me up and down, I turned to Carrie and she too had eyes transfixed on me.

"You really don't know do you?" Sophie was grinning. "I'm guessing you've read what the Internet and the local press has to say, not forgetting our two schools? The whole speech from the following morning's assembly was published in the press. What lovely words about me and what pitiful ones for you."

"The Internet was inconclusive, the press ... the papers." Carrie was stopped in her tracks. Spit ran down her cheek. Pink spit.

"I told you ... shhhhh!" Sophie growled.

"Sophie, for fucks sake, you don't have to be so fucking vile." I stepped forward to wipe off the phlegm.

"Would you rather it had been cum?"

"Jesus what the hell is wrong with you?" Carrie yelped. "Nick, I know you said she was fucked up, but this, this goes beyond even what you've described."

The chains rattled, Sophie came up at us off the bed, slipping on the tiled floor before the restraints took hold. Her breath stank, her sunken eyes, remorse free, evil eyes fluttered between us.

"They're going to let me out of here soon. And then I'll get you." She was bating Carrie. "I always take what Nick loves. It renders him ... vulnerable." And then she started to scream.

Instantly I heard the nurses working the locks.

"Say 'Hello' to Pauly on your way out," she scowled.

A few seconds later the door burst open. Two female nurses, middle aged, motherly types, came in. They gave Carrie a glare as they calmed Sophie down with soothing words and gentle strokes, whilst the lady who smelled of bleach, stood in the doorway and looked on.

"I think you're done here."

"Why the chains?" Carrie asked.

"Isn't it obvious?"

"I'd like an answer."

"She's depressed. At her wits end after what happened. She's missing her boyfriend, which shows just what a lovely soul she has, despite the fact he tried to kill her."

Carrie's face went a deep purple. "You still haven't told me. I said, *why* the chains?"

"She's been trying to kill herself ever since she came in. She wets the bed every night and gives herself all sorts of horrific bruises, the poor lass. They're for her own safety, she'd never hurt one of us - her heart is too soft, too loving. See what comfort we bring her."

"And she us," said one of the other nurses - Sophie's head, resting across her chest. It was then I noticed a newly painted pink cross above Sophie's bed.

"I'm sure soon enough and with the right medication, she'll be out soon."

"Soon," whimpered Sophie.

"We'll find you a lovely young man, deserving of your beautiful soul," said the third nurse.

I buckled, holding my stomach and tried desperately not to puke.

"She got to you too huh?" I finally managed as I brushed past the nurse in the doorway. She waved her hand as if a wasp was in her ear. Carrie tutted and followed me out of the cell.

"*Soon*," again came the voice from inside the cell.

CHAPTER SEVEN
Indecision

We, or rather Carrie, was bundled out of the main door of *The Asylum* into the fading light of the hospital car park. I managed to squeeze through the gap between Bleach Lady and the doorway just before she closed and locked it. Keeping us from all the misadventures happening inside. The cool, dim evening was a relief from the dark, dank inside. Sophie's cell was no more of a bedroom for the sick and needy as our relationship was for true love. Sophie had already inflicted her sociopathic skills and was worming her way out of detention through her own '*homiletic*' prayers. She had been learning all right, and now, now she was teaching. Her minions to the outside world were sure that *soon* she would be out. What did that mean for the world; her family; my family; Carrie; me?

Would she come looking? Would she wish to extinguish everything and anyone that linked us? Or would she simply let be and move on to her next victim; her next quest; her next new life? How would I get the answers then? She was hard enough to track down and to eventually confront this time around. People were protective of her. Weak-willed zealous nurses had given us less than ten minutes with her. What say of her new friends; new family; new lover? As much as I didn't want to go into the hospital to see her, I now wish I was back in there - bringing this to a close, finishing this once and for all. I was weary and felt that time was running out. Being so far away from the comfort of Jersey had taken its toll. I was more agitated and at a loss than ever.

Carrie's eyes looked up at me from her beneath her brow, "Maybe we should just go home?"

"I don't think I can ... "

"But I don't see ... "

"I need to consider what to do."

"Let's get some food and figure it out. C'mon you must be starving."

"No. But let's at least get far away from here." I could barely stand up.

"There must be a takeaway nearby?"

"You're spoilt for choice here. If you're feeling really flush there's even a pie shop." I climbed into the car, wincing as I sat down.

"We'll just pop into the first one we see. You look like d ... " Carrie coughed and started the engine. "Sorry," she mumbled.

.   .   .

The hospital hallway was visible only by moonlight. Each door I passed to the right, instead of numbers, had nameplates with fairy tale characters scratched on them. On the left and opposite, were their nemeses. The first doors had Little Red Riding Hood facing The Wolf, the second: Rapunzel's was mirrored by The Witch, the next: Cinderella and the Evil Step-mother and then at the final door to the right, the claw-like etching read: Needful Nick, and opposite: Sociopathic Sophie.

This door crept open, the familiar nursery-rhyme started and the small young girl was once again sitting on the floor slicing her wrists as she sang. A twitching afterbirth leading a bloody trail to a chained Sophie in a straitjacket. Her cunt exposed as she muttered the song. She looked at me as she finished the recital and lunged forward; the chains tearing from the wall as her teeth sunk into my neck.

.   .   .

"Cheeseburger or Chicken?"

I could smell something. Food maybe? I wasn't sure?

"Nick wake up, cheeseburger or chicken? Or we could have half each? I got chips too, and milkshakes. They only had vanilla left though, can you believe that?"

"I really don't think I want anything."

A new taste; earth, in my mouth, getting ever stronger.

My head remained busy with noises - scratches and clicks but the most disturbing remained the ever-present whispers, challenging what happened that night. Sophie's voice; Carrie's voice; my own voice. Every time I stopped to think, to concentrate, they rose ever louder. My head felt so thick and heavy that I wanted more and more to just lay down and go back to sleep, yet the terrifying visions when I closed my eyes, made this impossible.

"You've not eaten since ... "

"I've not eaten at all," I interrupted. "The one thing I did get down, came back up."

"Aren't you hungry? Thirsty?"

"I was. At first it's all I thought about. The thirst especially. Now I ... I guess I just feel full. Sickly full."

"Maybe it's just the stress of all this?" We broke eye contact and looked into our laps.

Carrie slowly got through the chicken burger. Pulling it apart into bite-sized pieces and finishing with the salad that had dropped out and into her lap. Each bite was interlaced with a slurp of milkshake, which gradually needed less and less effort. Finally, she scrunched up the packet and put both this and the empty drink carton into a brown paper bag. Each movement she made was in slow motion - delicate and precise. The unwrapped cheeseburger remained between us - a draughts piece awaiting its next move.

We were parked up in an industrial estate. The car was dimly lit by the large McDonald's drive-through sign a hundred yards away. There were two other vehicles, parked closer to the light and both articulated lorries. Other than that, the place was deserted; empty; cold. In the distance, one corner of St Dymphna's Hospital was visible - one window, leading to one cell, bathed in moonlight.

"Do you mind if I get a bit of sleep before driving us back to the port? As long as we leave here by 3am we should make it okay."

"No, that's fine."

"What is it, Nick?"

"Nothing, it's okay. Sleep and I'll wake you."

"Aren't you going to sleep too? I can set my alarm."

"I don't think I'm done here yet." I shifted, but still couldn't get comfortable.

"Nick, no. Seriously this time I don't think you should. There's something not right with her. Not right at all. In fact very fucking far from right."

"I told you that. *Sociopath*. Remember? We came up with this together. The research. You knew what you were getting into."

"I'm not sure I really did, Nick she's way beyond what I thought she would be, she looked ... *possessed*. There I've said it. She's pure evil, Nick."

"She was never quite that bad, not quite so obvious and never in front of anyone either." I considered.

"She wasn't even surprised to see you? What's that all about? She's knows you're dead, Nick. Where's the sense in any of this?"

"Do you not think I've been trying to figure that out? That's why I cannot leave."

"But what do you hope to achieve? Hasn't she already had her pound of flesh? We're safe in Jersey, she won't come there. You said yourself she'll start up another life here or elsewhere. Wherever. Let it be someone else's problem. Being away from Jersey, since we left, you've ... you've been less like you; your skin; the way you are; I'm scared, Nick. *Really* scared."

Not only did I feel like I was decomposing on the inside, something obviously was changing about me on the outside. I looked to the rear-view-mirror and she was right. My eyes appeared lighter, even in the dimness of the car, yet were set deeper. My skin, always of a good healthy colour had become pallid and was sagging slightly. My lips, cracked similar Sophie's, were not blood red, but had a dull, bluish tinge.

"And you think this will improve when I get home?"

Home.

"I'm petrified we won't get home unless we leave tonight."

"Believe me, I have every intention of leaving tonight."

"They will never let us back into *The Asylum*. You saw the way they looked at us."

"The way they looked at you, you mean? They don't even know about me remember."

"Oh God, Nick, this isn't good."

"I have to, you know that."

"At least let me come with you. I can open doors for you."

"No, not this time, I need to do this on my own. If the doors won't open, then I'll just have to improvise I guess."

Carrie started to cry.

I spoke softly, desperate to put her at ease, make her understand, "I can't let you come into contact with her again. I need to protect you. Protect your innocence. Finally it's my turn to stand up to her; alone."

Alone.

Carrie sucked in her lips. "Okay, I get it, I really do. I knew this time would come. But please ... do one thing for me before you go."

"Anything."

"Make love to me."

CHAPTER EIGHT
Nick and Sophie

We snuggled for a while, our naked bodies entwined. As Carrie shivered, her breaths grew deeper and I knew it was time for me to leave.

Let her have her sleep ready for the drive back to the port in just a few hours.

It was time for us to say goodbye, to part and go our separate ways. The final act of love-making had been the perfect end to a most unusual friendship. I loved Carrie and she loved me. I felt it like I never truly had with Sophie. The soft, tenderness of Carrie as I entered her, the shudder and look in her eyes made it all the more beautiful. I hoped she would always remember that moment, the time when it had been 'just us'. Oh how I longed for Carrie to have been the person I had met all those years before, and not Sophie. That I was finally sure of. How my life would have turned out, what I could've achieved and what we could have discovered, explored and experienced together. Fuck my life.

Fuck my death.

I turned to kiss her one final time on her salty forehead. As I did so, a single tear ran down her cheek to catch my own that had fallen onto her.

"I wish it had been you," I whispered, before turning quickly to get out of the back of the car and forcing my aching body onwards, into the rain that had started to fall. Although tempted, time and time again, I didn't dare look back.

I pulled my hands up into the sleeves of my jumper and hunched as the weather worsened. My head was buried into my neck but I kept my eyes firmly on where I needed to go - just as the storm clouds moved in. *The Asylum*, even from this distance looked increasingly sinister with each clap of thunder and associated flash of lightening. Sophie's cell was still the most visible, the one with the best view over the town and the one that could be seen in return. How long before she got out? Cleared of all blame? Forgotten about? Then, who would be her next victim? Who would she wrap around her finger and bleed off? I had to find out the truth and make it right. I quickened my pace.

I crossed the wet empty roads, which reflected the storm's electricity. The town that I grew up in, the one where I met Sophie and the place where I had died now seemed like a ghost town. In the short while I had been gone, the aftermath of what took place here between Sophie and I, had caused a concertina effect - a result of an overreaction to the press's derogatory view of the area. An attack on the society that called this place home. We caused this. *She* caused this. Riots and looting ensued and businesses I knew and loved became boarded up. Windows were cracked or missing altogether in the majority of the empty places that I used to dash in and out of with friends, often with a football at our feet. Nothing, especially in this darkness, seemed familiar or welcoming.

It was a Saturday night, not long after midnight. This place, when I was last here would have been thriving. The streets lined with drunken people. Girls in short skirts barely extending past their arse cracks. Guys with low v-neck t-shirts showing too much chest hair and bling. All cramming the streets as touts weaved amongst them selling tickets to clubs and bars, offering free drinks and more, anything it would seem, just to get them through the door. Then of course there were the shifty little weasels and too confident meatheads, stacked with more than just brawn, praying on the partygoers, selling them all sorts of legal and illegal highs for less than the price of a packet of fags from the local corner shop. But I would have preferred this to the desolation before me. Anything to muffle the whispers in my head.

A welcome bellow of thunder sounded and just behind the hospital, lightning struck. I inched ever nearer.

.   .   .

As the gates eventually came into view, the rain finally eased off and the storm clouds parted to allow the moon full rein on the place where Sophie now resided. A moments calm as I paced the walls looking for a way in, until stumbling across a recently fallen tree to scurry along and up over the wall. The embers still aglow within the dry, decaying innards. Somewhere in the distance, I heard urban fox cubs screaming.

I landed expertly the other side on sodden grass. The first day spent exploring the woods, a distant memory; the twilight hours spent on top of the shed, near forgotten.

I hunted around the hospital grounds, searching for another way in other than the main entrance. To the back of the building were two large fir trees and in the middle, a weeping willow. The light from the hallways of each floor, illuminating just enough to make out something not quite right. As I approached, the smell grew stronger and smoke drifted my way. It was a familiar if ominous smell.

"Took your time to come back." Sophie's voice cut through me. Chiselling my bones, clasping my heart and puncturing my soul. "You and your new girlfriend been fucking?"

The storm started again. A torrent of water instantly soaked me. Through the streams of water I could make her out fully. Bare, dirty feet. Creased, damp, nightgown that was once white. A face, not softened, even in this decayed light.

"How did you know I'd come?"

"You're way too predictable, Nick. Can't let anything lie can you?"

"How did you get out?"

"I'm not out, I'm just on vacation. *Garden leave*. Call it what you will."

"Won't they come looking?"

"Who? The night guard who I fucked to let me out here in the first place. You guys are all the same – so easy to intimidate, so eager to please a young girl who has no other way of getting relief. Too eager to please themselves more like, as they prey on the vulnerable."

"Sounds a little hypocritical to me."

"You're just pissed that even in this godforsaken place I'm getting some. C'mon I saw the way you looked at me in there. Why do you think your friend went so quiet? You've never looked at her like that."

"You're right. Thankfully I haven't."

"Whatever."

"How long have you got here ... outside?"

"As long as I need. I just tap, tap, tap our special tap on that door over there and he lets me back in. All hard and oozing with pre-cum no doubt. It doesn't take him long, especially if he shoves it in my ... "

"Stop, Jesus Christ stop!" My demands are firm enough to snap her away from her conceited descriptions and she starts to hunt for the butt of her dropped cigarette in the wet grass. As she shuffles on all fours in the dour light, it's clear she's wearing nothing underneath. My stomach somersaults and I look away, but not quite quickly enough.

"Like I said, all the same," she stepped forward and grabbed me hard between the legs, pinning me to the base of the weeping willow, holding me there, snarling at me until she looked down at where her hand was and gently released.

"Turned queer now have we?" she muttered as she walked around the base of the tree to other side.

"Not used to it are you?" It's my time to sneer.

"Bothered."

"Oh I think you are."

"Really? You have a lot to learn, dear Nicky boy. For every bottler that turns me down, there's another ten that will happily do me, at whatever cost."

"Sociopath!" I'd finally said it. "You're a sociopath, you don't care about anyone or anything. You lie to manipulate people into caring and doing anything for you, some even falling for you. Men, women any age."

"Words, Nick. Just words that make labels."

"Christ, Sophie what about your brother?"

"That dumb fuck should never have been brought into this world. A total embarrassment. I did him a favour, everyone thought that."

"No, Sophie, of course not everybody thought that. Only you thought that. Do you seriously have no repentance? No shame that you caused his death?"

"Inadvertently caused. People felt sorry for me you know."

"And just how convenient for you."

Sophie lit a second cigarette, taking a long drag before fixing her nightgown straight.

"Want one?"

"No. Not ever again."

"Suit yourself."

"You're not better than me you know?" She exhaled the toxins, "You're not."

"Funny you query it then."

"So you've labelled me, well done. It's all bullshit. You think you've figured me out, not that I care for any of this you know."

"Of this, I'm fully aware of."

"Course you are. So why are you here - you *dead freaky whatever the fuck you are?*"

"I can't be freaking you out that much?"

"Believe me, after being in here, the drugs they give you, the sexually aggressive guards. I've experienced worse things though; much worse things."

"Like what?"

"Nothing I care to talk about."

"Were you pregnant?"

Sophie flinched, taking a step back so she was in darkness.

"Was it mine?" I asked.

"I doubt it."

"But that last time we..."

"That was the only time *we* didn't use protection. Besides, it's only been a short while since then, how could it have possibly been yours."

"Just clutching at straws I guess." I looked down at my hands and then at my chest.

"Nothing left in this world of you, Nick. You should've walked away when you had the chance. Stopped the pestering; stopped the analysing; stopped trying to recreate me."

"I thought I could help."

"It wasn't wanted. Really, Nick I thought you were more intelligent than this."

"Then why did you even bother to tell me you were raped?"

She paused. "Isn't that what people do when they get together? Tell each other their secrets."

"Only it wasn't such a secret was it? Just how many guys did you use that opening line on?"

"What's it to you?"

"It's not true is it? I questioned it at the time and thought, no one could really be that ... cruel."

"Then why would you question it at the time?"

"It's not something you tell someone on a first date."

"Like I said, it's what people do when they get together."

"No, no, they don't Sophie. It's either a cry for help, and you've so adamantly insisted that you did not need help, or you ... "

"Or I what exactly?"

"Or you created that scenario to make me; others; think that you needed help. To manipulate them into believing that because something so horrific happened to you, that you are a defenceless little soul - desperate for someone to look after them; desperate for someone to love them and give everything to them. Guys like looking after girls. They like to feel needed, wanted and loved. And by you initiating a made up past, so harrowing, so invasive; that it only speeded up the process for the guy to fall for you, to protect you and to give up all of his secrets to you; ready for your own self serving sociopathic manipulation."

Clap ... *clap* ... *clap* came Sophie's hands. The scars on her right wrist, pink and raised, the left wrist, still heavily bandaged.

"I cut a little deeper than I intended didn't I?" She smiled as she examined herself. "You'll never know all the answers, Nick. I'm nihilistic. I looked it up." Again, smiling. "You fucking idiots think with your cocks. Why would any girl in their right mind not want to exploit this? Manipulate the lust that you mistake for love and turn it to our advantage."

"You're wrong, Sophie. From my experience, it's the other way around. Look at us!"

"Do you think you'd have really fallen in love me with so quickly had I not invented that story?"

Invented.

And there it was. Admission in all its glory. To hear it brought an instant rage but with that a subsequent calmness; a realisation; an acceptance.

Resolved

It was minutes before I spoke again, "I would have fallen for you. You didn't have to make anything up for me to love and care for you. You just had to be you - that's how relationships work."

Sophie reacted instantly, "I don't buy it. You know what I am now and I can see the utter distaste, the disgust; in your eyes."

"How do you expect me to feel? What you put me through when we were together - the bullshit you fed to keep me understanding your excuses. The things I let you get away with and yet I always took you back. I knew you were no good but I had never loved anyone before. One love, one life, one person to live out the rest of your life with. That was my fairy tale!"

"You should know that in every fairy tale there is an antagonist. A witch ... a warlock ... a wolf." Again, smiling.

Fairy tales.

The rain, even heavier than before, was now accompanied by thunder.

"You do know you'll never be truly happy don't you?" I insisted.

Finally her mouth dropped. So I pushed on, "You have an inability to love anything, anyone, other than yourself. You're vacant - empty inside and as you say, *completely nihilistic.* How that doesn't bother you I'll never know. A life without love, well that's not really a life at all is it?"

Sophie looked away and backed into the shadows the trees provided. She lit another cigarette. I looked behind me to the door to the building, but still, we were alone. Her hands were visibly shaking.

She inhaled and spoke through the escaping smoke, "They're not my real parents."

"If this is another ... "

"No, no it's not," she interrupted. "This is something I've never told anyone before."

There was sorrow in her voice and for the first time in all our conversations I didn't doubt the legitimacy of what she was saying.

She continued, "I never knew my parents. My mother died at birth and my dad gave me up. Paul was excitable when he told me the story about them."

"How did he ... "

"He overheard my parents one day - my adopted parents that is. Paul was their own and I guess they wanted a girl and someone that wasn't like *him*. I was available and ticked all the boxes."

"Did you ever try to track your dad down?"

"Funnily enough he was in Jersey, both my parents were from Jersey and that was where I was born." I stepped towards her. "Don't bother to try and find him though, he died not long after mum." Sophie backed against one of the trees and picked at the scars on her exposed wrist.

"Then why did you never tell that story instead?"

"That's intimate - too painful. Both stories are about the loss of innocence - I just subbed one for the other."

I took another step towards her.

"Do you love her?" she asked.

"I do." And took a step back.

"I see the way you look at her. It's the way you used to look at me."

"The same way all the guys looked at you?'

"No. No you were very different. You were the only one that really did try. I guess in my own way I did love you."

"Then why not let the right one in?"

"How many relationships do you see in the world around you that work - I mean *truly* work? People have the passionate stage; the excitement; the first dates; the lust; but then this all wears off and we simply become complacent with each other. Why the *fuck* would you want that?"

"I loved you and continued to love you. Passionately love you I mean."

"Yes but only because I kept it *fun*."

"If that's your idea of fun ... "

"Oh come on, Nick. No-one wants a mundane relationship. That's what keeps the excitement and interest going."

"The excitement of not knowing where your girlfriend is? Who she's sleeping with? Whether she's going to come back diseased ... pregnant?"

"It would appear there was never any baby, I just guessed there might be. Although I find the prospect of boys becoming fathers laughable. However, some people seem to crave the responsibility, even if they didn't know it yet."

"That's a cruel game to play."

"No crueller than telling someone you've been raped when you hadn't. It's interesting that you seem even more dismayed about my *pregnancy* than my *rape!*"

Now it was my turn to look away. The prospect of Sophie carrying my baby had been a glimmer of hope.

"It was personal. A situation between us. And besides, you weren't raped."

"Even so, you seem to have been keen to take on ownership of my child regardless as to whom the father was?" she questioned knowingly.

"Yes, a child needs to feel loved. I couldn't image it would get any from you." I blurted.

"What because I never loved you?"

"You just said in your own way you did! You're constantly contradicting yourself. You know what, I think that maybe you actually did but then just got scared and so you rebelled against me. Ignored me. Imagine what that sort of behaviour would do to a child!"

"Again, Nick, a reluctance to realise the truth. Telling a boy you love them makes them do unspeakable acts of wonder for you. I must have been in love dozens of times," she gloated. "People in love are so desperate aren't they? Can you see why I refrain?"

"To live and not truly love ... well, you've never really lived at all." I reiterated.

"Give up on this psychobabble bullshit, Nick. That sounds like something you'd find in a fortune cookie." Sophie dug the heel of her left hand into her temple, wincing as she did. "Besides, I've already had one kid, it was only a few weeks old but that was enough."

"You had one? I thought you had the pregnancy terminated?"

219

"That's what I mean. I had to change my story a little though."

"Your story? To whom? About what exactly?"

"To the nurses, about the baby."

"Go on."

"Well I thought about having it, you know my brother's offspring, then he would be sent away and wouldn't be affiliated with me any more."

"What the fuck? Where are you going with this?"

"Like I said in the hospital."

"About sleeping with your brother? Seriously?"

"If you want to put it like that. We only did it a few times. I was so fucking pissed off that I had to look after him one week when my fucking selfish parents went away, that I thought I might as well have some fun. Besides ... I was curious."

"I don't think I want to hear this."

"Why not? You seem intent of finding out about all the juicy stuff - you can't have it both ways."

"Well first off I don't think it'll be true. But if it is then ... "

"Oh it's true all right, you said yourself in the hospital."

"I don't recall what I said."

"Let me put it this way. I could describe to you, every inch of his body ... "

"Leave it. I'm not interested. It's time I ... "

"I called him into my room, I was naked on the bed, lights on and I had my legs open ready for him. I was playing with myself and quite aroused at the thought actually."

"Ok enough, this is fucking disgusting."

"Oh is it now? How so?"

"He's your brother."

"Not by blood he isn't, although I did bleed when he fucked me the first time. I'd seen his cock before when he was showering, it was fucking huge! I said I was curious ... "

"Fuck, no I don't want to know. Enough now. Please."

"But I thought you wanted to know everything?"

I stayed silent, so she continued.

"He came in his pjs when he saw me lying there. Star Wars pjs, can you fucking believe it? Anyway, I had to go over and start him all up again, although within a few seconds he'd cum again. In my mouth this time, but at least he was getting geographically closer. Maybe I shouldn't have licked him clean after the first time. But it didn't take him long to get hard again, although he came a third time when I tried to get a condom on him, so I just rode him bareback instead. Fuck I thought he was going to break me he rammed it in so deep. I came quicker and harder than you ever made me."

Dismissing as best I could, for what I'd heard, I enquired for clarification, hoping for any kind of inconsistency, "So how long did this go on for?"

"Well that week we barely left the house. It was fun to play with a virgin and a fucking stupid one at that. He knew absolutely nothing; about anything. I knew it was a bit sordid but that's part of the fun isn't it?"

"It's wrong, Sophie. That's what it is. You can't dress it up any other way."

"We weren't doing anyone any harm."

"Other than to the baby you created."

"Foetuses don't feel things, not even at 32 weeks."

"You what?"

"Like I said - I thought about keeping it. Would've been fun and then I wouldn't have had to work and stuff. Loads of girls do it."

"How? That's not even legal is it?"

"What would you know about it?"

"But that's almost full term, you must have been ... "

"Quite fat yeah. But I explained to all the nurses and the doctors I had been raped by a retard and they did what I asked."

"This doesn't make sense, how can they do this without your parents' consent. Surely there are legal forms?"

"My teacher did all the paperwork."

"The one you slept with?"

"Again, with the *sleeping* word! Yeah, I *slept* with him. If his wife had known he was having a baby with another girl he'd have been taken to the cleaners."

"But you said ... "

"I covered my bases. Told him it was his, you know. Like I did with you."

"Answer me one thing."

"I'm an open book, you know that."

"What is it you get out of all this?"

"Well, I got an *iPod* from my dad," she was counting on her fingers, "Some designer clothes and a watch from the teacher ... hmm what else. Oh yeah I also caused my brother's death, kind of. I got a lot of sympathy for that. That was *nice*."

"That was *planned*?"

"Yeah. You were there weren't you? With John." Her eyes lit up.

"You knew?"

"Of course! So anyway, my original plan didn't work and my *pretend* parents didn't send him away after he took advantage, and can you believe they actually threatened me, saying it was all my fault. I'm the girl for fuck's sake and only little at that. He's a fucking big cunt, it was obvious ... well it should have been obvious ... "

"So how did you *construct* the whole thing?"

"Well it was right that he had a heart defect. Of course he did, he was built *wrong*. What do you expect when you allow something like that to come into this world?"

I should have been shocked but I wasn't.

She went on, "Whilst fucking me a few times I thought I'd actually been able to give him a little help in that direction. And there was once or twice when I got him to the point of where he went blue, but then he'd come back around and manage to fight me off. So I'd try again and again until one day he stopped wanting to do anything at all. He took a liking to Special Spacker instead."

I searched rapidly to try and tie that name to someone real.

Familiar.

Finally, I recalled: "Stacy?"

"Was that her name? I dunno? Anyway she was another fucking flid. Can you believe he chose her over me?"

From memory, neither Paul nor Stacey had anything especially wrong with them. Not in the way that Sophie was describing. In that very moment I realised how she saw the world. It was a competition for her, one big game in which she played many parts. Those in her circle were also *played*.

"Wait," I started. Sophie began nodding enthusiastically. "Wasn't that the girl who ... "

"Hung herself? Yes! Yes it was!" She was clapping; *actually clapping*. "Right here. Both of them right here, I got them an absolute classic didn't I?! And they did it to themselves. All that needed to be done was to walk Spacker here before school one day, tell her the story about what was inside me and hand her the rope. You know how emotional these mongs get. Abusing her for weeks on end about her mum who used to work in that ... in this place, *might* have helped; *might* have set the ball in motion."

Things becoming clearer ... the voices ... waning.

"And I thought it was me."

"Thought what was you?"

"That was to blame for your suicide, for pushing you into a corner. God if only I knew all of this."

225

"Would've saved yourself a journey huh!"

"Do their ghosts not follow you?" I said in a dreamlike state.

A memory?

"What was that?"

"Just realisation."

"Realisation"

"You're everything I hoped you wouldn't be, but *more.* Much more."

"I told you to stop prying didn't I?" She crossed her arms.

Smug.

"Okay you win. There is truly no hope for you." I confessed.

Relief. Acceptance.

Finally I admitted, "You are truly lost."

I dwelled on my next move. I had come here to end her and now, being here I had absolutely no idea as to how I would do it? How I *could* do it? I needed to feel angry with her, yet all I felt was pity. She was indeed far beyond what I thought she was. I looked back towards the horizon and thought how long before Carrie made the dash for port and her return home. "It's time for me to go."

"Fine, whatever. You're already gone, remember?"

"Actually I don't remember ... and to which you're well aware."

Smiling again, it was Sophie's turn to take a step forward. "What I'm not sure of though is why I, and that twat you came with, are the only one's that can see you?"

I refrained but I could feel my blood boil.

"The staff nurses at the hospital mentioned how strange for a girl to come all this way on her own, without any reason. They initially thought she was a friend, and then panicked and thought she was press for some college newspaper or indeed writing social media about the trials and tribulations of teenage suicide. The latter was actually what they settled on and I could sense that they were remorseful for letting her in here - less for their own jobs of course, more for how it might affect me."

"You have them wrapped around your little finger."

"All three had been sexually abused. Maybe it's why they worked in care? To be with other people who are mentally unstable - just like them."

"And of course you told them your *fable*."

Sophie shrugged. "Like I said: people endure to me because of it. Anyway, I'm done with me now. Let me reiterate what I'm getting at. They saw Carrie, but they *did not* see you."

"I'm done with you too, unless you have any further revelations for me. My dying for example. Care to share this one last story."

Sophie eyed me through her hair.

"What do you see Sophie? Seriously. When you look at me? A ghost, zombie, human? You're the only one that can see me that knew me before."

Sophie studied as she circled me. Taking her time. Watching me grow ever agitated. I looked to my wrist for a watch that had never been there.

Finally, "I see you. But then I don't see *you*."

"Stop with the riddles, I don't have time." I looked again to the horizon.

"I think you're too frail to make it back to her. Too frail for the ride home, even if you do." She folded her arms. "Soon you'll be gone though. Gone from this world."

"And why does this please you so?"

"When you're gone, you no longer will have a voice." She came forward so her mouth was close to my ear. "And then all of my secrets will be safe."

I felt one hand on my back and another push sharply forward into my stomach.

"I only hope that I don't have to try and kill you a third time." She backed away and as she did we both looked at the blade in her hand.

In another time and another place; I took a step back and stumbled, instantly grabbing my stomach from where the blade had penetrated. Sophie was there, screaming at me against the backdrop of the kitchen sink. Her limp hand spewing blood from its open wrist. Her other hand pointing towards me, extended by the six-inch blade that she held. The blood from it was a brighter red and as she stabbed at me again I felt it partially slice through the joint of my thumb as it buried deep inside me. When her hand retracted this second time, it held no knife. I instantly went for the handle, turning as I did towards the front door of her house, removing the blade from my torso just as I stepped out into the bright, bustling, street, watching people gawp at me before fixing on Sophie and her screams. Only when I dropped the knife did they rush to her. My last vision was that of three large men pining me down and another kicking the utensil into the gutter.

"Why won't you fucking die?" Sophie screamed at me, the light of the upstairs windows of the Asylum, glistening off the knife.

I looked down, expecting to find a shirt wet with blood; but nothing. I lifted my top and saw a pale, heavily-stitched puncture-wound I hadn't noticed before. My stomach retched - instantly aching with the memory of what had truly happened that day.

She was still brandishing the knife, slashing at the empty space in front of her. "I couldn't let you tell the world about me ... secrets are *everything*, Nick."

I looked again towards the asylum.

"No-one there to help you, Nick. No-one can even hear or see you. The fucking freak you've now become. A ghost without a voice; without a body; without a soul."

I sank to my knees, the earth pulling me downwards, consuming me inch by inch. The cool, damp ground, getting ever colder the further it dragged me in. Crippling me as it engulfed my legs, crushing the last breath out of me as it rode up onto my chest, clawing at my throat.

Sophie was standing over me, goading me; her eyes wild; her skin as pale as ever and her ink black hair matted against her face. The nightgown covered a twisted, skinny, yet muscular body and was stuck to her, revealing every naked contour. She waved the knife, taunting my withdrawal from the world and was the epiphany of pure evil.

"No, Nick, not here...." a familiar voice, a tight grip on the back of my neck, "not now!"

"Get away from him you bitch!" The grip loosened and I started to slip back into the abyss.

As my eyes shut and the soil muffled multiple screams, I was once again lifted, more timidly this time, in gradual stages until I was completely free from the earth. Carrie was on her knees alongside me. Her hand holding her stomach; she was covered in blood.

CHAPTER NINE
Nick and Carrie

"Can you walk?" Carrie asked.

"Can you?" I cross-examined.

"We have to, before *they* come." She was pointing at the door to the asylum, where a scruffy guard was adjusting his belt as he rushed into the yard, another was shortly behind.

We managed to pull away, behind a tree and around to the side of the building. A third person joined the group, a female nurse this time. All were shouting to Sophie ... to each other.

"Do something, you're the nurse!" said the first guard.

"What the hell is she doing, out here?" she replied.

Then there was pushing and shoving. The first guard fell into the disturbed mud that had almost consumed me.

Whilst getting up he knelt on the knife before secretly slipping it into his pocket.

"Get her inside. Quick get her inside, she's not breathing," said the nurse. "Get the doctor! How the hell did she get out here? Answer me!" The guards looked at each other but neither replied.

Carrie waited until the door was shut and the garden silent before nudging me to move on. Both of us, managing not much more than a crawl, made it to the surrounding wall of the asylum where the natural climbing frame had recently been created. Somehow we helped each other up over the branches and to the opposite side where Carrie's parents' car was parked at an angle, tightly against the brickwork, the driver's door still open, a dim light shone inside. A drop down of no more than seven feet was easily made, despite the lethargy I was feeling. Carrie was my main concern. She was still holding her stomach, her right hand hadn't moved since her fight with Sophie, but the deep red that her shirt had been, was now a more diluted pink. She was at least finding it possible to stem the flow.

"We need to get you to the hospital. I'll drive, I know the way."

"No fucking way, Nick. We only have one way out of this. I'm not doing time for her." She looked down at her wound and repeated. "No fucking way." Before getting into the drivers side. "Get in the back and lie down, you can barely stand. I can do this. I can get us home."

"To Jersey?" I asked.

And just before I closed my eyes, "Of course ... Jersey," came the reply.

.   .   .

I rubbed the heavy crust of tear-filled sleep from my sticky eyes and focussed towards the seascape. We were driving rapidly away from the harbour, already in Jersey.

"Wakey, wakey Mr Sleepy Head," said the girl.

Who?

I rubbed my eyes harder.

Rub, rub, and rub.

Carrie?

"We're here!"

"Carrie! Shit, how long have I been out this time?"

"About twelve hours. I got a good nap myself on the boat. How're you feeling? You're looking better!"

234

"Tired, but okay I guess. Wait, my God, what about you?" I crouched forward between the seats to look at her stomach.

"Guess I wasn't as bad as I thought. It's kinda crusty so I haven't examined it yet." Carrie looked down at her shirt. "We'll get home and then I can have a proper look."

"I think we should get to the hospital first."

"Why?" she looked back at me, "Oh my God are you okay?"

"I meant for you, you numpty." I insisted.

"Ha! Sorry. You do seem better than before. Maybe sleep was all you needed?"

"Hmmm. Maybe? So are we going to the ... ?"

"No, Nick, not yet. We need to get our shit together. They're bound to come calling."

"I'm ... I'm really not sure what happened?"

"Me either. It's like a dream you know, but not a dream. I can't believe we got away."

"I don't even think they saw us. Can you believe that?"

"It was really dark ... and really raining!"

"But still ... "

"I think they were more concerned with covering their own arses ... did you see him hide the knife ... that guard?"

"I did."

"Gimme your phone, I'll have a look."

"I tried ... no service on the boat and then I ran out of charge. We'll have a look when we're back. There's bound to be something on the news. There must have been CCTV. Nick, oh God, what are we going to do?" .

"This nightmare isn't ever going to end is it?" I stared out of the window. We had already left the dual carriageway and were meandering north through woodland. "Even if she's finally gone?"

"Is she? Is she really? I sense that she is, I mean ... oh fuck, Nick I don't know how many times I cut her?" Carrie was sobbing. "I can't believe how much she struggled, so I just kept going until ... until she went limp. She was heavier when she did that. It was strange. I was holding her, and then ... and then I couldn't anymore."

I leant forward and put a hand on her shoulder.

"I hope to God that's it."

"You do know I had to don't you? She was trying to kill you! I *had* to."

"I know." Carrie had done by herself what I had intended to.

"She would have tried again, in the future I mean. I couldn't bear to see you having to constantly look over your shoulder. She would've come again and again."

"I think the damage was done the first time," I muttered.

"But she stabbed you again I saw her do it. I was on the top of the wall looking for you, I *saw* her do it."

"I felt her do it," I started, "but yet this time, it ... I don't know ... it didn't ... "

"I saw you hit the deck. Fall into the mud."

"The ground was pulling at me. You know. Like it was swallowing me up. And I ... I saw what happened ... the first time. I didn't try to kill her." I took a deep breath. "As she started to slice her wrists, she then turned on me. That was her plan all along. She just didn't mean to cut herself so deeply. She wanted them all to think that I had slashed her to make it look like suicide and then killed myself."

"She didn't think it through so well did she?"

"She didn't need to. Her ability to manipulate means she always had the upper hand. Her cold collective personality ensured, as always, that she had been the victim. A short spurt in a mental institution would ensure *she* got all the sympathy."

"But the nurses, they knew she did it to herself. Didn't they?"

"There were always flaws in her stories. If you asked enough, eventually you got slightly different answers. That was her only weakness: inconsistencies. Those who spent enough time with her - the one's that were truly concerned, would eventually pick up on them - if they listened hard enough. The nurses had still made excuses for her, just as I had first done."

We pulled into the driveway at speed and immediately cut the engine, crawling the last few feet silently. Carrie gave me a wink.

"Time for the backlash!" Carrie looked at the clock on the dashboard just before it faded out. It was almost 6pm. She removed the sticker from the windscreen that showed we had been on the ferry and popped it into her purse.

"I'll meet you at the entrance to the woods in half an hour ... if I'm not grounded. I need a shower."

"But what about the hospital?"

Her look said it all but she offered more, "I'll charge up the phone quickly and then we can see what's what. At least in the woods we'll be harder to find if *they* come."

"Okay, half an hour," I reiterated. She turned to kiss me quickly but we stayed connected until I was ready to let her go.

"I think you must've eaten some of that mud you fell into," she smiled, before studying me more seriously. "Make it fifteen minutes instead okay?"

"Okay. Good luck."

"You too."

"I'm invisible, remember."

Carrie turned back towards me and gave me another kiss, just a lingering peck this time. "Not to me you're not." Before exiting the car and going towards her front door. She fumbled with her keys in the lock, before becoming so irritated she pulled away. "They must have left the keys in the other side, shit that means they're in. I'll go around the other way and try and sneak upstairs. See you in a bit."

Watching Carrie go out of sight brought on the fear of isolation again. Back in England, when I left her in the car, I really thought I might never see her again, but she had come back for me; rescued me, and in the process, killed Sophie. But what now for me? For us? I guess I would find out in fifteen minutes.

CHAPTER TEN

Carrie

I barely had to wait thirty seconds let alone fifteen minutes to see Carrie again. She was wailing - desperation rife in her voice as she sprinted across the driveway towards me, flicking up gravel against the car we'd just arrived in.

"Nick, they've gone, they've gone!"

"What are you talking about? What do you mean?"

The house, it's ... empty," came the reply - only just audible through uncontrolled sobs. She flung herself into my arms.

"How can it be empty, we've only been gone *one* night?" I looked to the house, at the perfect mirror image to my own and started to lead her back towards it, disbelieving.

"Th... the door, it's l...locked."

I diverted us towards the side of the house, practically running now until I found the open window Carrie had used and peered into the lounge. It was the smell that hit me first and I was instantly reminded of woodwork class: the shaved chippings, glue and wet paint. As I clambered in, I saw that the place was empty, completely bare. But that wasn't my main concern. As I helped a reluctant Carrie back into the room I sensed something so very, very wrong; this house had *never* been lived in.

CHAPTER ELEVEN
Carrie's House

I wandered through her home and although I had never been here before, I knew the set up, for the interior was exactly the same as mine. Carrie was much more urgent, breezing through the rooms muttering to herself as she did. Hurriedly she went upstairs, and I went after her, knowing where she was heading. In a room exactly the same as my bedroom across the driveway was a bare shell, recently painted and with unfitted carpet. There were no curtains nor ... nor shutter type blinds.

I took a quick couple of steps to the window and squinted upon the house opposite - my house, before instantly rushing back out of the room.

"Wait, where are you going?" asked Carrie.

"It's not there." I yelled, as I launched myself down the stairs, "My room, it's not there."

"How can it not be ... ?"

"I can see into the room from here, the wall opposite, it's ... "

I rushed to the front door of Carrie's house, shaking the handle before going back out the window we came in. I sprinted across the driveway and went straight through my own front door without hesitation.

CHAPTER TWELVE
Nick's House

Everything was as I remembered it. I scanned around looking for anything that was irregular before running up the stairs two at a time, skidding to a halt in the doorway to my bedroom. I heard rapid but lighter steps come up behind me. Carrie rested her body against mine, her chin on my shoulder.

"What does all this mean?" she asked. My throat burned as I looked into the empty room: no bed with blue sheets; no pillow with blue cases; no poster on the wall.

"It's like we never existed," I replied, gazing through the window that looked out over the driveway.

In the middle of my own room, looking around it: there were no marks on the walls where the poster had been, no indentations on the newly laid carpet and no sign than it had ever been ... my bedroom.

"Your room Carrie, what was it like? I mean before now. I never saw it." My voice echoed.

"Just a standard seventeen-year-old's room I guess. Small, double bed, a desk full of trinkets and chargers for items I no longer had, some posters on the walls. Everything I ever wanted or needed was in that room."

"Yeah mine was pretty much the same. In fact it was the exact replica of what I had on the mainland."

We spent the next hour searching the rest of the house looking for evidence of my existence. Carrie spent most of the time in a daze - pacing back and forth, her head in her hands.

"Everything feels like a dream," she reiterated. "I'm trying to remember what else was in my room, but I can't."

"Carrie, your phone!" I shouted.

"Shit, yes!" She pulled it out of her pocket and shook it. "Do you have a charger? M...my things, I don't..." She started to sob.

I ran to her, almost knocking her over as I threw my arms around her. "Oh fuck, sorry." I quickly pulled back, looking down at her stomach. "We need to get you to the hospital ... still need to ... " Her shirt was dry, white, clean. I launched my hands towards her, ripping open the lower buttons. Her tanned, smooth skin was free of any damage, not a scratch nor even a bruise. "But you ... "

"I know, I ... I thought I was a goner." She sat down on the floor and held her head in her hands. "Am I dead? Did Sophie kill me too?"

I raised my t-shirt, but the heavily-scarred and hastily-stitched wound remained. Carrie looked up to catch me studying it and shook her head slowly and pitifully.

"We need to get online," I said. "Maybe then we'll know what happened to your mum and dad. Find where they are? If they're looking for you?"

"Charger?"

"There might be one in the box under the stairs, I'll take a look. Sophie had taken mine off me after I put hers ... " I couldn't be bothered to finish the sentence.

I pulled out the box from under the stairs which contained the usual items that didn't have a home. Manuals for items we no longer had, cables for an analogue TV and thank you cards from weddings. At the bottom of the box were my old school reports and one solitary album containing pictures of me when I was a kid, of which only the first few pages were filled. I flicked through the photographs of me with mum and dad within hours of my birth; one with me in a buggy; another with me and my godmother, and finally came to the last photo of me with a football in the back garden of Grandma's old house, just a couple of miles away from here. I must have been about four-years-old. At the very bottom of the box were my more recent GCSE results. My life summed up in just a few items stuffed in the cupboard under the stairs.

"Anything?" Carrie made me jump as she came up behind, unnoticed.

"No, sorry." I closed the box up and slid it into the darkness at the back of the cupboard.

I turned to Carrie, "Give me your phone and I'll see if it can charge off one of the radiators." We exchanged a look, "I saw something about it on telly."

She handed me the phone.

"Carrie," I whisper, "it's on!"

"Wait, what?"

"It's on 3%!" I showed it to her, waving the screen in her face.

She snatched it from me, "But that's imposs ... fuck, there's no reception."

"The woods! Quick, let's get to the woods - there's always a signal there."

CHAPTER THIRTEEN
Carrie's Parents

Carrie was quickly out of the door into the humid late summer evening. I followed behind, surprised in my ability to keep up. A far cry from the night before, when I had barely been able to crawl away from *The Asylum*.

We jumped down from the rise and headed for the tree where we had previously looked up the sociopathic Sophie Pemberton on the Internet.

Carrie stopped at the trunk. Breathing heavily, she waved the phone in the air and within seconds it gained a signal.

"How much ... "

"Still at 3%," Carrie interrupted. She aggressively typed away on the phone, concentrating hard with each page she reveals, before moving onto the next one. Less than a minute passes before she slumps down at the base of the tree and urgently hands me the phone.

I notice it was still at 3%.

"Nothing is coming up!" she starts, crying. "Nothing."

I looked at her and then back at the phone. In the search bar, Carrie had simply typed:

Carrie's missing family Jersey.

"Okaaay ... let's try something else." I then was about to enter Carrie's surname, but stop. I glanced to the battery life, still 3%.

"What is it?" she asked.

"I think we should search on your surname."

"Excellent ... good ... good thinking." She looked at me, open-mouthed and I gave her the same look back. Carrie reddened.

"Okay let's try your address instead then. I'm Woodland Rise, St John, I don't know the number but you must be one or two. We're the only houses here for fuck's sake."

Carrie was looking into the distance, her eyes filled with tears.

"Carrie?!" I prompted.

"Try *one*." Her reply is solemn - without emotion. "Then try *two*."

I sighed and began to type the addresses. Eventually I found a court notice which stated:

Transaction 9983.09/14 - Sale of Woodland Rise by Le Cornu Properties to undisclosed buyer - £625,000

I searched for a second property but nothing. Finally I searched under the transaction number to find out if there were any more details and instantly achieved the following result, again from a court notice:

Transaction 9984.09/14 - Sale of land by Le Cornu Properties to undisclosed buyer - £325,000 see ref 9983.09/14

The mobile still showed the battery life at 3% when I searched for Le Cornu Properties.

Suddenly the screen was awash with links to newspaper articles and public debates. People were enraged that a house and land had finally been sold, when it was promised it would always remain the sole and exclusive property of *Jersey Heritage*. One of these links was to a *Facebook* page titled: *Alice and Philip Edinburgh*. I reinstated my account and viewed the page in its entirety. Looking intently at photos of the couple and then at

Carrie who was still sulking. She caught my gaze and shuffled over, pulling the phone down from my chest into full view.

"You found them!" she yelled, her excited eyes turned to mine before quickly sinking and dropping back to the phone once more and the first photo on their page. It was a scanned copy of the inside back cover of the *Jersey Evening Post*:

You are now with Alice and your heart is whole again. Rest In Peace, Philip.

CHAPTER FOURTEEN
The Encompassing

We sat without talking, whilst I continued to scour the Internet. Carrie's head was on my lap and although I had tried to comfort her, she had insisted that I keep looking for more answers. The sun had lost its way behind the trees, heading rapidly towards the horizon.

Carrie finally spoke, "Alice and Philip Edinburgh. So I'm Carrie Edinburgh?"

"I guess you are." I shrugged. "What's your first memory of your parents?"

"There isn't one," came the nonchalant reply.

"Well then just tell me things you do remember about them." I wanted a conclusion to this.

"That's just it. There isn't any memory at all."

"You don't ... but you only saw them yesterday?"

"I can't recall anything? That is ... anything other than us."

"You remember meeting in the woods that day?"

"Yes, you were asleep. I woke you. That's the first thing I ... "

"The driver's licence! Carrie you have your mum's driving licence!"

"I do! Oh my God I do!" She checked her pockets and then her purse. "I must have left it in the car. Shit." Carrie was up already, "Be back in a minute. You stay here and keep searching."

With the mobile at 2% power I hastily began looking for more clues. Anything that could explain what was going on. I'd heard of people having imaginary friends but imaginary parents? That was just too bizarre. Carrie had obviously been through some trauma herself. That would explain this. All of this. Wouldn't it?

You've fucked her up too.

I searched for **Carrie Edinburgh, Jersey**, but nothing. There were a couple of names turning up in ancestry sites, but none more recent than the 1960s. I brought up the *Facebook* page and started to go through the scores of tributes left to Alice and Philip. All the photos of them were digital

253

reproductions of Polaroid's or 33mm style, 6x4 printouts on what looked like exploration trips around the world. They looked not much older than us: in love; happy. They looked like nice people.

Yet there was no mention of a Carrie.

Finally I decided to request myself as a member to the page and was quickly approved. More information was suddenly available and upon reading, I instantly got up and ran for home. This was all fucked up. The phone lost its signal and flickered at 1% battery power.

As I got to the base of the rise I hastily began climbing - fearful I was now well and truly alone and would forever be. The roots slipped through my hands and the supporting mud failed to hold as I tried to clamber up. I was panicking - making the task impossible as the sun started to set. The dark creatures of the woods were coming to life and I was consumed with trepidation that they were finally ready for me - to take me the last mile, into the deep thicket, to my grave. I watched as the black, elongated wraiths edged ever nearer so in one last attempt, using every ounce of effort, I climbed the vines one last time. Grabbing clumps of rock and tree and digging myself into any foothold, I inched ever nearer to sanctuary before eventually lifting myself up and ...

Snap, snap, snap.

Tumbling backwards into the realms of the gorse below, I found myself staring up at a purple sky. My memory of a shed roof and broken ankle, all too familiar. Awaiting my fate, the woods whooped and hollered around me.

CHAPTER FIFTEEN
The Realisation

I closed my eyes and thought about the last few days. About how much had happened and couldn't believe this was how it would end. I looked back at the phone, at the comments made regarding Alice and Philip Edinburgh, their estate, their daughter and about ...

"It's gone, it's all fucking gone, the car, the house ... the fucking house! How could it just disappear?"

Imaginary parents and now an imaginary house.

Carrie jumped and sat down next to me, grabbing my shoulders. "How can it all be gone?"

The creatures retreated.

Stalking.

Waiting.

"My house too?" I queried.

"No, not yours, although your parents are home and their car is back. I saw them through the kitchen window. So I waved and knocked on the glass, then I tried the front door. They ignored me. Can you fucking believe that? I couldn't get in so I shouted and banged on the door but they never came!"

Carrie had done little else but sob the last few hours. My loss of life and interaction with my parents had drawn little emotion from me. My relationship with Sophie had, I thought, left me devoid of empathy. Certainly this was true of myself but for Carrie, well, I loved her and I wasn't sure if she could take what I had to tell her. Wasn't sure if I could take it? Watching her trying to get her head around the truth. How could I do this to her?

The solution was provided for me.

"I want answers, Nick. There's so many questions, my head is busy and I'm so, so scared I'm losing it."

Déjà vu.

"Okay," I started, "whilst you were gone, I found out *everything.*"

"You did?" Her eyes: doe-eyed; childlike; vulnerable.

"This will be a lot for you to take in," I cleared my throat. "Stop me when you've heard enough."

"Just *tell* me." Her voice: cold; desperate; forlorn. She brushed away the damp, tear-filled hair that clung to her cheeks. I had *never* loved anyone like this.

"Those *were* your parents: Alice and Philip, and they *are* both dead."

Carrie's eyes refilled but she motioned me to go on.

I took a deep breath.

"It would seem that *Le Cornu Properties* have held the estate for your parents, ever since they ... passed and that they've recently sold it on ... I guess ... to my parents."

"I've got a touch of amnesia, that's it! Maybe I was in the same accident as them? That would explain everything," she nodded. "I remembered living here, so I came back. Simple."

"It's not that simple I'm afraid."

"We really need to find out who looks after me now, they'll be worried and that's not fair to them, after all ... "

"Carrie ... Carrie! It's *not* that simple."

"How so?"

"They died seventeen years ago."

.   .   .

Carrie looked ever more pensive.

"There has to be some kind of explanation - to all of this, " she said. "You've got to give me more than that, Nick."

"There *is* more." I admitted.

"Well then tell me!"

I couldn't word it any better, "Your dad committed suicide."

"Oh fuck, no."

"Carrie it gets worse, please prepare yourself for this. You know I'll always ... always try to be here for you."

"What? What can be worse?"

"Your mum, well, she was giving birth to you and things went wrong, horribly wrong. She died during labour and your dad ... well he just couldn't live without her."

"M ... My m ... mum died because of me? My d ... dad too?"

I couldn't go on.

"Oh God, what? Where d ... do I live? Who looks after m ... me? It must s...say?" Carrie looked about three-years old.

"I'll look after you, I promise."

What happened to the truth?

"N ... Nick, the answers. P ... Please."

259

We were both shaking uncontrollably and the tears wouldn't stop for either of us. But I owed it to her to carry on.

"It wasn't you. You ... you were ... You're not to blame."

Something shifted in the woods. I jumped - ruffled by the distraction.

Here they come...

"How? I c ... caused this. Their deaths ... I ... I'm ..."

"You didn't," I snapped, getting in quickly before her point of no return. "The page was set up on what would have been your mum's 50th birthday. They were obviously very much loved as it triggered a release in many people - emotional outpourings from friends and family reminiscing about your parents - seventeen years after their passing ... of *your* passing."

"What?"

"I'm so, so sorry."

"Wait, what? I'm dead too?"

"It says so here. A few people have mentioned it."

"W ... what?"

"You died, Carrie. It's all here."

"What do they say?"

"That things aren't always meant to be."

"What? Me? My family? All dead? That was *our fate?*"

260

"Not exactly. Just that some people are sacrificed for others."

"What are you not telling me?"

"Sometimes things are better left unsaid. Sometimes ... not knowing is better."

Hypocrite.

"No. You need to tell me what you're hiding." Carrie had stopped crying. Instead becoming increasingly agitated.

I did need to tell her.

"Your parents were well respected here in the island, almost a celebrity type status, but unlike mine, in a good way. They did a lot for the island and for the environment. They did a number of talks in schools and to the public, including tourists. It says they were both zoologists who, after many years of exploring, had returned to Jersey, where they were both born, to work at the conservation park here. They had assisted in the births of many rare animals and everyone was delighted when they announced they were expecting their own ... children."

"W ... wait, ch ... children?"

"You were a twin." I nodded, taking another breath. "You were the first to be born, but you were stillborn, starved of oxygen and therefore much smaller and weaker than ... "

"Oh fuck, Nick, no."

"Sophie."

CHAPTER SIXTEEN
Quietus

I pondered how much more Carrie could take. Her parents were both dead and Sophie, the reason for our friendship, the reason I was here, and the cause of my death, was her twin sister. Our whole world was no longer real but at least I'd experienced some of it - seventeen years of it; seventeen more than Carrie.

I risked her sanity by explaining her death, as she had done mine, not so long ago:

"The doctors say you never took a breath and that their efforts were focussed on the stronger twin. Your dad though, well he apparently told reporters that you had been neglected and your mother was screaming at the doctors to save you. The second baby was coming but feet first. Your father demanded they save your mother and not the second baby, he could see it was ripping her apart. She died whilst your dad was holding you in his arms. Your mum's last breath christened you: 'Carrie'."

The girl that I loved sat opposite me and I could offer nothing of any comfort.

Distraught; disturbed; dead.

Finally came the realisation, "I'm like you?"

"Yes. But in truth ... you never really existed. Not here, on earth, outside of your mother." This she needed to understand, to comprehend.

"So I *never* even lived?"

"It wouldn't appear so," I confessed.

Carrie looked into my eyes, studying me intensely.

"But how do you explain the boat? England? *The Asylum?*"

"How can I explain any of this?" I questioned. "You and Sophie had a bond and I guess I did too. I did love her and she did kill me after all. Maybe that's it - we're connected."

"She should never have existed. She killed us - all of us."

As much as I understood the complications surrounding the birth and that Sophie couldn't be blamed for what had happened, she was still responsible. Her father had branded her evil and had completely lost the plot after the deaths of his wife and first daughter. Not forty-eight hours later he had taken his own life, having never held Sophie. Instead, a family in the UK adopted her: a Mr and Mrs Pemberton who had a young son with learning disabilities. They were warned against trying for another child for fear of repetition. Instead they were offered a child who was far, far worse.

"How did we get there?" Carrie questioned.

"To where?" I asked.

"To England, to Sophie?"

"Perhaps we imagined it." My blood ran cold.

"Then she's not dead?" Carrie looks down at her shirt. "Quick check the internet ... "

"It's probably died." I lifted the phone and was surprised to see it again at 3%.

I searched for St Dymphna's and before I got the chance to type any more, the screen was filled with news articles from the last 24 hours:

'St Dymphna's comes into question again after latest tragedy'

'Hospital staff criticised for negligence'

'Local girl is latest to die in The Asylum'

And there are many, many more. All of which name Sophie Pemberton as the deceased. The phone's battery flickered to 2% and illuminated brightly to ensure we were no longer in darkness.

Carrie looked at me, "Thank you. I feel strangely comforted. I couldn't go on with not knowing. Those voices, those horrible voices ... "

"You heard them too?"

"Not anymore, they've gone. You?"

"Just ... silence." I forced a smile.

"I guess we'll never have *all* the answers."

"I suppose sometimes it really is better; the *not* knowing," I admitted.

"So it's just the two of us." Carrie figured.

"The way it should have always been." I confessed.

We then stood up and walked to the place we first met, before snuggling against the base of our tree.

The woods around us had come alive once more: the sun's rays filtered through the trees, the birds sang and I could hear the sound of running water; I imagined that this place would tell stories of the nymphs and fairies that sheltered under toadstools when the rain started.

THE END

266

EPILOGUE

The hospital had asked for it to be kept out of the papers but the jealous tribe of night-workers at *The Asylum* had been accusing each another so vehemently, and to such an extent, that word leaked out. It would appear that the night-shift had a rota and not just one to man the halls. Sophie was able to get out each evening, sit under the weeping willow, and smoke; and talk. She spent a lot of time talking to those voices in her head and the staff were keen to give themselves a break - and their own little bit of peace and quiet - snoozing after an against the wall ejaculation into the girl herself.

When they had observed her going about her usual ritual that night, only did they make a beeline for her once she had drawn the knife. In their haste to get to Sophie, they saw her stab at an empty space several times in front of her, before turning the knife on herself, inflicting multiple wounds.

Despite how frail she was and the amount of injuries sustained, Sophie survived for many more hours. Eventually her body could fight no more and she was finally declared dead at 7.30pm - about the same time Nick and Carrie had entered the woods searching for a signal.

The coroner insisted that the angle of her wounds were at the extremes of those possible which one could inflict on themselves but hospital staff and DNA testing all provided conclusive evidence - that there was only one person involved: Sophie Pemberton. A note, written in the first person and in Sophie's own handwriting, confessed to everything she had done in her life, including the murder of Nick.

The police could only speculate how this letter was sent from Jersey, the day after her suicide.

On Nick's eighteenth birthday, and as they would do every year, his parents laid flowers at his gravestone. They would however, save three single flowers for the family grave alongside, covered in moss.

ABOUT THE AUTHOR

David Sellars was born in Jersey, Channel Islands where he still resides.

He was educated locally before attending Nene College in Northampton, where he studied Sociology and Sport - writing a dissertation on football related violence. He then studied fiction and playwriting with The Open University before a chance opportunity led him into the local tourism department. Here, he wrote copy for the official website, whilst managing PR for the UK, Dutch and German market, and was also involved in Sports Marketing.

Further study ensued and he gained a Tourism Marketing Diploma before successfully completed a Masters Degree in Professional Writing from University College Falmouth. He has two short stories in print and **Quietus** is his first full-length novel.

Genres include dark romance, horror, thrillers, crime, fairy tales, travel and comedy.

To write whilst travelling is his constant aspiration.

You can find David at: www.davidsellars.com
Email: d.sellars75@gmail.com Twitter: @Calm_Seas

Made in the USA
Charleston, SC
25 August 2015